EMERALD

Mage

OTHER BOOKS BY DOROTHY DREYER

Phoenix Descending

Paragon Rising

Cauldron of Ash

Crimson Mage

Copper Mage

Golden Mage

COMING SOON IN THE
EMPIRE OF THE LOTUS SERIES

Sapphire Mage

Amethyst Mage

Diamond Mage

COMING SOON FROM ROSEWIND BOOKS

Christmas in Silverwood

EMERALD

EMPIRE OF THE LOTUS
BOOK FOUR

DOROTHY DREYER

Emerald Mage
Empire of the Lotus Book Four

Copyright © 2020 Dorothy Dreyer
Edited by Amy McNulty
Cover design by Sora Sanders

Paperback ISBN: 978-1-948661-44-7

Published July 2020 by Snowy Wings Publishing
PO Box 1035, Turner, OR 97392

*To those who believe in justice
and speak up for those who've been held down*

A foreboding prophecy. A lost empress. And a battle to determine the fate of the world.

In the arduous war against the dark god Kashmeru, the elite mages have managed to track down half of the magical daggers. But the enemy isn't far behind.

Leading the shadow army, the dark mages have won battles of their own, and the Lotus empress is still under Kashmeru's control. But mysteries are unraveling that could help the elite mages gain an advantage--if they can survive long enough to fulfill their legacies.

When I stand upright in the wind,

my bones turn to dark emeralds

— James Wright

The legend goes …

The ancient deity Kashmeru knew only one true love—the Lotus empress Lakshmi, who in his eyes possessed all beauty and grace the universe could hold. Their hearts called to one another, a hold so strong that neither one could deny the bond. But Lakshmi knew that Kashmeru's spirit was not pure, for an evil dwelled within his soul, a wickedness so corrupt that it could destroy the universe.

And when she denied him her love, destroying the universe was the very thing he vowed to do.

Throughout the centuries, their reincarnations were drawn to one another, but the outcome was always the same: Lakshmi would never give Kashmeru her heart.

To put an end to his constant chase, the Empire of the Lotus defeated Kashmeru and sealed him in a tomb using mage powers, where he would remain trapped …

… until the Council of the Seven could secure the blood of the Lotus empress to set him free.

THE SEVEN HOUSES OF MAGES

Crimson: earth, stability, survival, security.

Copper: water, ice, pleasure, guilt.

Golden: fire, willpower, shame.

Emerald: air, wind, heart, love, grief.

Sapphire: throat, sound, truth, lies.

Amethyst: vision, sight, illusions, secrets.

Diamond: spirituality, emotion, virtue, integrity.

One

Loni Saengkaew stared at the emerald stone on her wristband as the car climbed a hidden road headed uphill. The stone caught the light of the moon, reminding her of the many nights she'd spent fearing the fulfillment of the prophecy. Things had been a mess since the destruction of the academy, but the last few months, in particular, had turned her life upside down. She sucked in a sharp breath through her nose and crossed her arms, clenching her hands into fists and tucking them in at her sides

In the driver's seat, Penny spared her a glance, the flecks of purple in her eyes sparkling from the streetlights. Out of the four mages in the car, she and Penny had been together the longest, venturing as a team through the post-Eradication chaos to get to where they were now.

Loni had been squatting in an abandoned Linq factory for almost three months when Penny had found her. It was just one of the many places she had camped out while on the run. Penny had simply shown up, in her dark purple leather jacket and knee-high, black boots, telling Loni she needed to come with her. Thankfully, Loni had remembered Penny from the academy, but they hadn't been in touch in years, so it had been a surprise to see her. As the elite Amethyst mage, Penny had used her power of insight to find her, but because Loni had moved around so much, she hadn't been easy to track down.

The trees flanking the small road they were driving on began to decrease in number. Up ahead, at the top of the hill, the surroundings cleared to reveal a beautiful temple. Loni leaned forward and took in a deep breath, as if inhaling the sacredness of the temple, hoping for comfort. The truth was she was a wreck inside. Physically, mentally, and, most of all, emotionally. The only thing keeping her going was justice. She'd promised herself she would see this through. She would destroy Kashmeru herself, if she could.

The car in front of them—the one they'd been following—pulled into a carport. Another car was already parked there, along with a motorcycle that she recognized.

When they parked, Loni looked over at Yuki—the diamond mage—who removed a hairband from her wrist and swept up her shoulder-length, auburn hair into a messy bun. Yuki yawned, and Loni almost made a joke about it being past her bedtime but refrained. Yuki had heard it all before. At seventeen, she was probably the youngest elite mage to have ever existed.

The four mages emerged from the car simultaneously. Kamal—the elite sapphire mage—stretched his arms above his head and slightly arched his back. As he kicked out his long legs, he looked around at his driving companions, his ever-present, cocky grin twisting his lips to one side.

The four passengers from the other car were already waiting for them. Jae—whom Loni knew well—signaled for them to follow and headed toward a door seemingly guarded by a white, stone elephant. He looked almost the same as she'd remembered, with his short, dark, hero hair and his square shoulders. He did seem a little more worn for the wear, but the rugged look suited him.

For being so close to the busy road at the bottom of the hill, the temple was quieter than Loni had expected. She had to admit, though, that the pink sandstone columns and white marble floors were a far more pleasing aesthetic than the murky, soiled, and rotten-egg-scented places she'd been used to camping out in during the past couple of years.

Up ahead of her, the crimson mage—Mayhara, she remembered—ran her hand along one of the stone elephants' tusks before she entered the temple door. There was no denying she was beautiful. Her flawless creamed-caramel skin contrasted nicely with her thick, dark hair. Jae placed a hand on the small of Mayhara's back as he followed her inside. Loni wondered, with an itch of jealousy, how long they'd been a couple.

"Come on inside." Shiro—the copper mage—held up the dagger, which he'd wrapped in a red cloth. "I'm going to store this somewhere safe and catch up with you."

Inside, the temple's ceilings were at least ten feet high, and the marble floors were polished. It didn't feel like a temple. The feeling Loni got was more like it was an extravagant home, filled with comfortable furniture. Though, she wasn't too familiar with many homes decorated with elegant stone statues of various deities. A gentle breeze floated in behind the mages as they entered the building, carrying with it the pleasant scent of jasmine.

An archway to the right of the main entrance hallway led them to a spacious kitchen. In the breakfast nook, sitting at a small black ceramic table, were two older people. Loni recognized the woman as Darshana, her guru from the academy. The man, however, she'd never seen before.

Darshana eyed the group coming in and jumped to her feet. Her hands flew to her mouth, trembling slightly. Her white hair was pulled back into the long braid Loni was familiar with, and she still had stunning skin for someone her age.

"I can't believe it." Darshana walked over to the four new mages and took each of them by their hands, one after the other. One by one, they bowed to her in greeting.

The salt-and-pepper-haired man at the table stood. Loni had expected him to be taller than he was, probably due to the sense of importance he seemed to convey. He certainly dressed like someone important. He bowed as he approached them. "Judging by the amount of jovial energy flooding the room, I assume these are the other elites we have been looking for. It's a pleasure to meet you. I am Mr. Kitaro."

"He's a Sacred Key," Jae explained. "A keeper of one of the magic daggers."

"Cool," Kamal said, flipping the bangs of his stringy black hair with a jerk of his head.

Jae raised a brow at his comment, causing Loni to bite the inside of her cheek to keep from laughing.

"I'm Apinya. But everyone calls me 'Penny.'" Penny bowed to Mr. Kitaro.

"Ah. *Apinya*." Mr. Kitaro nodded. "It means 'magical powers.' How fitting. You have wonderful specks of purple in your irises, matching your amethyst mage powers. How perfect."

Penny's forehead creased for a fraction of a second.

"Thank you?"

Next to her, Kamal bowed again while sticking his hands in his pockets, typically combining an air of respect and apathy in one move. "I'm Kamal, and I guess I'm the new elite sapphire mage. Penny just found me a week ago to let me know, so I'm still trying to wrap my head around it."

"Nice to meet you, Kamal," Mr. Kitaro said.

Since she stood beside Kamal, Loni decided to go next. She raised her hand and then stuck it behind her back. "I'm Loni. Emerald elite."

"One of my best friends from childhood was an emerald mage." While Mr. Kitaro smiled, it didn't reach his eyes.

Loni refrained from questioning whether or not that friend was still alive.

Everyone's gaze then went to Yuki. She looked around with her wide eyes as if unsure of what to do. Relief seemed to wash over her when Penny spoke up for her.

"Yuki is the diamond elite."

"I should probably be shocked by such a young elite," Mr. Kitaro said. "But diamond mages are so rare that I imagine the former elites who were… *eliminated* by the Pishacha were few in number."

Yuki's only response was to drop her gaze as she nodded, tendrils of her long, auburn hair slipping from her hairband and falling in front of her pale, narrow face.

"You all look famished," Mr. Kitaro said.

"I'll make more tea," Darshana said, heading for the stove and grabbing the kettle to fill.

Kamal raked a hand through his hair. "I mean, I could use a shower and a beer if we're offering things."

"Why don't I whip up something to eat?" Jae's gaze fell upon Loni before he headed for the cupboards.

"I'll help," Mayhara said. Her smile told Loni she hadn't caught the look Jae had just given her.

Though Loni couldn't be sure what meaning might have been behind that look in the first place. Because the last look he'd ever given her had been one of disappointment.

They'd moved into the dining room so everyone could sit

comfortably around the table and eat. Penny moved her food around her plate but hadn't taken a bite. Though *bibim gooksu* Jae and Mayhara had whipped up smelled delicious, with the scent of spices and vinegar filling the air, Penny simply had too much to divulge to the group and was in no rush to eat.

"So you saw my Linq number in your head?" Jae asked, reaching for the water carafe to fill his glass. "I didn't know amethyst mages could do that."

"Normally, we can't," Penny said.

"It's a highly unusual skill," Darshana added.

"Good thing, too." Kamal snorted. "Otherwise, amethysts everywhere would be stealing credit account numbers and winning lotteries on the fly."

Yuki gave him a disapproving look.

"It took a lot of meditation," Penny said, ignoring Kamal's remark. "And when I finally pinned it down, I contacted you right away."

"Via a mysterious message." Salina pointed her chopsticks at Darshana. "Which actually led us to one of the daggers."

Penny shrugged. "I figured it would be diligent to kill two birds with one stone. Plus, I didn't want to identify myself in the message, just in case it was intercepted."

"Which it might have been," Mayhara said. "Would explain why the Pishacha showed up."

"So you know where the other daggers are, then." Shiro narrowed his eyes as if he were trying to calculate some major mathematical equation.

"Yes." Penny set down her chopsticks. "The Pishacha have three of them."

Shiro almost choked, sputtering as he tried to clear his throat. "Three? I thought they only had two."

"Yeah, we counted two," Salina added.

"One was acquired recently." Penny dropped her gaze, as if disappointed in herself. "They got to it before we could."

Darshana put a hand on her chest, taking a deep breath. "Yes. Yes, you are right. I'd felt a disturbance, but I believed it to be Huojin's downfall."

Salina frowned. Penny could feel Salina's sorrow over her friend's demise as if it were her own loss.

Mr. Kitaro bowed his head and closed his eyes. "Another Sacred Key has fallen."

It was quiet for a moment. And then Mayhara spoke up. "They have three, and we have three. There's one left.

You know where it is?"

Penny nodded. "I do."

A tingling sensation traveled in a repeating wave through Penny's head. Her senses were on high alert. Someone was approaching the temple.

"We should probably—" Jae stopped mid-sentence when Penny abruptly turned her head and stood from the table.

As she proceeded from the dining room toward the front door, she could hear the others following her.

"Penny," Loni called. "Should we be afraid?"

Penny didn't stop walking, her boots clunking along on the marble floor in a consistent rhythm. "I'm not sure. Something is wrong, but I can't tell."

Searching her mind, she found something blocking her insight powers. It had to be magic; that was the only thing that made sense. But what was it? She could just make out the faint glow of the various-colored light behind her as the other mages prepared themselves for a possible fight. But Penny couldn't sense that they were in any danger. Unless her senses were betraying her.

She opened the door.

There, not ten feet from where she was standing, was

a young woman with smooth, pale skin and dark, unkempt hair hobbling toward the door. On one arm, she propped up an older woman with scraggly white hair.

"Amalia?" Darshana said from behind Penny. Her eyes were on the older woman.

"Help," the young woman said. "She's dying."

Two

Shiro ran forward to the other side of Amalia and wrapped her arm over his shoulder. He immediately felt the dead weight of the old woman leaning on him. Amalia whimpered with every step she tried to take. Karina—Amalia's granddaughter—squared her jaw and grunted as they worked together to get Amalia through the front door.

"What happened?" Shiro asked.

"It was a dark mage." Amalia's voice was hoarse and

weak. "He did something to me. It feels like poison is running through my veins."

The rest of Amalia's words were lost beneath a barrage of coughs. Karina and Shiro carried Amalia to the living room couch and gently set her down. Amalia gasped in pain as they released her.

Darshana, Mr. Kitaro, and all the mages gathered around, baffled at this new development.

"How did this happen?" Darshana asked, sitting herself down on the coffee table in front of the couch so that she was eye level with her friend.

"I was out collecting herbs." Amalia scrubbed a trembling hand over her face. "They cornered me."

"The Pishacha," Karina added.

"Oh my God," Loni exclaimed.

"Why did they corner you?" Shiro asked.

"They wanted me to help them."

"With what?" Shiro shook his head. "Why you?"

Amalia shifted on the couch, wincing. "Kashmeru was sealed in a tomb by the empire, but they used a witch to bind him there magically. In order to keep a being as powerful as a god locked in a tomb, they had to use a powerful spell performed by an even more powerful witch."

"That's a lot of *powerfuls*," Salina whispered.

"And because it was sealed by a witch," Amalia said, "it can only be opened by a witch."

Kamal scratched the back of his head. "So what's that have to do with you?"

Loni smacked him on the arm. "She's a witch, dumbass."

Kamal cleared his throat. "Y-Yeah, okay. I just, uh, figured that out."

"Not just any witch." Karina looked around at the group. "She's probably the most powerful one in the world."

Shiro nodded slowly, putting the pieces of the puzzle together. "So that's why they cornered you. They wanted you to do the unbinding spell."

Mayhara crossed her arms. "And the dark mage attacked you because you refused."

Amalia opened her mouth to respond but fell into a fit of coughs. She could barely nod to answer Mayhara.

Karina rubbed her grandmother's back but looked up at the mages. "Of course she refused. And in return they tried to kill her."

"No. No. They didn't try to kill me." Amalia waved a feeble arm in the air, catching her breath. "The dark mage who attacked me—he was rail thin and had green, spiky hair—he used a power on me I didn't know a mage could have. It was as if needles were penetrating my skin and injecting me with a burning, itchy acid. I could barely breathe, and I lost control of my body and fell in the mud. He pushed me down with his boot and told me I had seventy-two hours to change my mind or else his magic would kill me. Then he and his Pishacha bodyguards disappeared. They left me writhing in the mud."

Karina's brows drew together, her mouth set in a frown. "She'd been gone longer than usual, so I went looking for her. When I found her, she told me to bring her here. The dark mage's magic has been in her system for about eight hours now."

"Amalia, we're going to do everything we can to help you." Shiro took her hand in his. "You saved my life. I'm going to do whatever it takes to save yours."

Yuki began to pace, her eyes far away. "I don't understand the Pishacha's plan. If you still refuse, and they let you die, they're out a witch anyway."

Amalia put a hand on Karina's knee. "That's another

reason I wanted Karina to bring me here. You need to keep her safe."

"We're not giving up on you," Darshana said. "But of course, we'll keep Karina safe."

"Thank you, Darshana." Amalia bowed her head to her.

"So, theoretically," Jae said, sitting in the chair next to the couch, "they could find another powerful witch to do the unbinding spell."

"Hope there're not too many of them around." Kamal held up his hands. "No offense."

"It's not as simple as that." Amalia grunted as she shifted, leaning her elbow on the arm of the couch. "There are a couple of other things required in order for the witch to harness enough power for the spell to be in full effect. The same elements required when they sealed Kashmeru in the tomb, but… reversed, in a sense."

"What things?" Yuki moved to the floor, sitting next to the coffee table and tucking her legs beneath her.

"When the tomb was sealed, there was a celestial event—a full solar eclipse. The powers of the seven elite mages at that time were combined and channeled through the Lotus. And a powerful witch performed the binding spell. To open the tomb, the Pishacha need a celestial event—"

"The comet," Mayhara said, sitting on the arm of Jae's chair.

"The council of the seven would draw the power from the Lotus through her blood using the seven daggers, and a powerful witch is needed to undo the binding spell." Amalia held up a finger. "But not every witch has knowledge of the spell."

"But you do, right?" Kamal asked.

"No," Amalia answered.

"What?" Kamal scoffed. "Then I have to ask again, what does all this have to do with you?"

"Shut up, Kamal," Loni whispered.

"The spell is in a grimoire," Penny said. She had been quiet during the entire exchange, standing at the back of the room, listening.

"What's a grimoire?" Salina asked.

Penny let out a sigh. "It's a book of spells, usually very ancient. Not something you'd like an enemy to get ahold of."

"So we just have to keep the grimoire away from the Pishacha." Salina looked around, hopeful.

"Where is this grimoire?" Darshana asked.

Both Amalia and Karina shook their heads.

Amalia wrung her hands. "It is in a place called The Archives. A hidden place made by witches where important books and items are kept safe. I was there once when I was very young. But to protect me, my mother performed a charm that made me forget its location. I have no idea where it is."

Mayhara stood and turned to Penny. "Please tell me you know where it is."

Penny shook her head. "Not exactly. It's protected by magic, like Amalia said."

"Okay," Loni said. "But if we don't know where it is, it's highly unlikely that the Pishacha will be able to find it, either. So it's moot. We've just got to make sure to get all the daggers so they can't perform the ritual."

Kamal shrugged. "That does seem like the most logical plan."

"All right, then it's settled." Jae nodded once. "Let's get those daggers."

Three

It was three in the morning when they finally decided to turn in. The men had generously offered to clean up the dinner dishes, and Darshana brought Karina and Amalia to a guestroom on the ground floor to stay in. Amalia could barely walk, but Karina proved herself to be pretty strong. She had to have been, since she'd rescued her grandmother from the swamp to bring her to the temple.

"There are a few more rooms upstairs," Mayhara said.

"Plenty enough for everyone. Salina, will you help me get the ladies settled while the boys finish up?"

Salina fought the small churn in her stomach. "Sure."

Mayhara led the way upstairs, bringing the young women to the first empty room down the hall. Salina followed behind them. She couldn't be sure, but she felt as if Loni had been avoiding making eye contact with her. After all these years, could she really still be angry with her?

"Here's the first room." Mayhara opened the door and took a step back so the others could look inside. "They're all pretty much the same."

"I'll take it, if no one minds." Yuki covered her mouth as she yawned. The dark circles under her eyes were a dead giveaway to how exhausted she was.

"Good night, Yuki," Penny said, placing a hand on Yuki's arm. "Sweet dreams."

"Night, everyone." Yuki gave them all a tired smile, her eyes half-closed as she wandered into the bedroom and closed the door.

A few steps down the hallway, Penny turned to Mayhara. "She's been through a lot. Two diamond elites were killed by the Pishacha before she became the new elite. She knew she was next. When the Imperial Police asked her to come in to answer some questions, she knew it was a setup. She could feel their emotions and knew they were hiding something. She made them think she was cooperating, gave them the slip, and escaped. It was only a matter of hours before her parents were slaughtered in the prison camps."

"That's awful," Salina whispered, a hand on her heart.

Mayhara frowned in silence. Salina wondered if it was because her parents were still trapped in the prison camps.

"She's tougher than she looks," Penny said. "But she's still young, and I can't help but feel responsible for her."

Mayhara stopped in front of the door to another empty room. "You seem to have adopted a sort of mother role to the others."

Penny shrugged and let out a sigh. "I had to find them, and I knew their lives would never be the same. As the cornerstone of that pivotal turn, I just feel—"

"She's been amazing," Loni said. "Like, really there for us. At least, she has been for me."

"I think it's something that I've always felt I needed to be able to do." Penny pushed her hair behind her ears.

"My parents were killed in a car crash when I was young, so I had to take care of myself for a long time. I think I relayed that into an almost maternal instinct for those in need."

"You're awesome at it," Loni said softly.

Penny gave Loni a small smile and reached out to squeeze her hand. "I'm about to drop right here in the hall, so I better get to sleep."

Loni pointed to the door across the hall. "If that one's available, I'll take it."

Salina couldn't help but notice that Loni had directed the statement to Mayhara. She hadn't imagined it; Loni was avoiding looking at her, much less talking to her.

"Yeah, sure," Mayhara said. "Sleep tight."

Salina rubbed at her shoulders, not sure how she felt about Loni's clear dismissal of her. They walked halfway down the hall before she realized Mayhara had been speaking with her.

"I'm sorry. What?" Salina bit her lip. "I was spacing out and didn't hear what you were saying."

"It's okay. We're all really tired. I was just saying we might have a shot, now that Penny is here. If she can track down the rest of the daggers, the Pishacha won't be able to fulfill the prophecy."

"Right. Yeah. I think we might actually have the ball in our court for once."

Mayhara studied her face. "Are you all right?"

"Yeah. Sorry." Salina shook her head. "I just got a little flummoxed around Loni. I wasn't expecting that kind of reaction from her."

"What do you mean?"

"You didn't notice the tension between Loni and me?"

"Sorry. Maybe I'm still on edge because of everything that's happened tonight. The battle on the cliff, the appearance of the other elites, and Amalia showing up poisoned on our doorstep—my brain hadn't even taken it all in yet." Mayhara looked over her shoulder before continuing. "What happened? Why is there tension between you?"

Salina opened her mouth to answer but couldn't bring herself to dive into the story. Not at three in the morning, anyway.

She crossed her arms. "It's a long story. Probably shouldn't get into it in the middle of the night. I think I'm just going to turn in. Darshana's probably going to have us training before the sun comes up, and my battery is on empty."

"Same here. But I'm here if you need to talk."

"Thanks. Good night, Mayhara."

Mayhara gave her a nod. "Good night."

Four

Naree splashed cold water on her face, the droplets trailing down to her forearms as she stared at her reflection. She couldn't quite remember how they'd gotten back to the mansion. But she'd grown accustomed to the lost time and blackouts in her memory. Kashmeru had always been there—at least audibly—to let her know everything was all right.

Only this time, he hadn't spoken to her yet. Deep

down, she could feel his rage. It was so strong, it shook her bones. And she understood his anger.

She had failed him.

She raked her thick, long, dark hair away from her face and tried to stop her bottom lip from trembling.

A softer voice inside of her—Lakshmi's loving voice, which was her own—told her to be strong. As the reincarnation of the Lotus empress, Naree was very powerful. She was, to her core, a strong leader, the sovereign of the Empire of the Lotus. Revered. Respected.

Yet Kashmeru was her undoing. The feared god was the darkness to her light, and he had control over her.

He'd asked her to acquire the arcane daggers needed to set him free from the tomb where he lay imprisoned. And she had failed.

There were seven daggers. She had three. The most recent face off with the elite mages was not successful. She'd been so close. She could have taken the dagger she'd been after away from the elites. Instead, she and the shadow army were ambushed. They'd been outnumbered, outwitted, and ultimately lost the dagger to the elites. The elites now had the upper hand, and Kashmeru knew it.

She took a deep breath and waited for his words. He loved her. She knew this. It was pure fact, centuries old. But to suffer his silence when she knew he was furious with her was something she couldn't endure.

As frustration tore at her, she pushed herself away from the bathroom sink and headed into her bedroom. Finding nothing but silence, she made her way downstairs.

The mansion's lounge area was a lavish room with a sixteen-foot ceiling, tall windows, and an enormous fireplace. The large, oak, double doors we accented with colored glass panes of amber and violet. Between the ivory statues and plush furniture, Naree should have felt like pampered royalty. Instead, she felt like a child about to be punished.

The murmur of voices caused her to turn toward the terrace sliding doors. She took in the sight of Bhutano waltzing in, speaking in low tones with three of the dark mages. She perked up, anxious to hear what they might be discussing, especially since Bhutano was the only other person Kashmeru spoke to besides her. He was Kashmeru's messenger, after all. His right-hand man, so to speak.

When their eyes met, Bhutano stopped speaking, holding a hand up to signal to the dark mages to halt the conversation. The dark mages pressed their lips together and eyed Naree as they continued to follow Bhutano through the lounge and through the oak doors to the mansion's conference room.

Bhutano cast her one last glance before closing the doors and leaving her in the room alone.

Naree crossed her arms and swallowed back the lump in her throat. She felt as if her stomach was turning inside out. She knew Kashmeru was mad, but she could only imagine what he had expressed to Bhutano for him to have given her that look of disapproval. She could barely hold back the tears as her insides soured, as if they were filling with acid. She plopped down on the couch and rubbed at her arms, biting her lip as she pondered what she could do to make things right.

Five

Loni opened her bedroom door to find Penny standing in the hall, waiting for her.

Loni held back a curse. "You'd think I'd be used to that."

"Good morning, sunshine. Darshana has requested our presence in the courtyard."

"This place has a courtyard?" Loni stepped into the hall with a scoff and closed the door behind her. "Not that I'm ungrateful. It was beyond wonderful to sleep in a bed that big and that comfortable after all the hellholes I've spent nights in."

"It's a nice change." Penny looked away from her as they walked.

"What is it?" Loni asked.

"Sorry?"

"I know that look, Penny. There's something you're not telling me."

They descended the stairs in silence. Loni waited patiently, hoping that giving Penny space would allow her to open up.

"I can't see it." Penny stopped at the bottom of the stairs. She turned to face Loni but still didn't look her in the eyes. "The day Kashmeru is released from his tomb. The vision won't come to me."

"But that's good, right? That means it's not going to happen."

"Not necessarily. I don't see anything past when the comet reaches the tomb. That could mean anything. It might be that our fates haven't been decided yet. It might also mean nothing exists beyond that point."

Loni's eyes widened. "Wow. Penny, you really know how to lighten the mood. Are you going to tell the others?"

Penny wrung her hands. "Not yet. I want to see if the vision comes to me… eventually. I'll meditate some more, and we'll see if it does."

"And if it doesn't?"

"Then we'll need all the luck we can get."

Shiro wiped the sweat from his hairline with a towel, catching his breath after the morning's training session. Though Darshana had been generous enough to give the mages an extra hour of sleep than usual, she'd pushed them extra hard today as well.

He had to admit, though, that it had been thrilling to observe the new mages using their powers. It had been years since he'd participated in a proper combat training with all the houses of mages, and he'd forgotten how magical it was. At one point during the training, he had aimed ice pellets at Loni. She had masterfully used her air power to whip them away from her. They'd zipped through the air in Salina's direction, and if Salina hadn't been so quick to use her heat shield to block them, she would surely have been hit.

"Hey, nice work out there." Kamal took a swig of his water bottle and gave Shiro a wink.

"Thanks. You too. I think my ears are still ringing from that sound blast you created."

"Cool, right?" Kamal crossed his arms and leaned against the archway of the meditation room. "You know I can control the pitch? I could make an entire song if I wanted."

Shiro eyed Kamal, who was smiling to himself as if pleased with the praise he lavished on himself. Didn't he know there was a war going on? Not that Shiro wanted to be a downer, but he felt as if Kamal was only interested in being in the spotlight.

"I'm going to go take a shower," Shiro said, making his way toward the hall.

"Can't you just water blast yourself or something? Save some time?"

"I'm pretty sure this clean-up requires some soap."

Kamal laughed as if Shiro had told him the funniest joke he'd ever heard. "All right. Catch you later, then."

Shiro held back from rolling his eyes and ventured

into the hall and toward the stairs. As he walked by Amalia's room, he heard a continuous mumbling. Curiosity got the better of him, and he slowly pushed open the door, which stood slightly ajar.

Amalia was in her bed on top of the covers, lying still with her eyes closed. If it weren't for the rise and fall of her chest, he would have worried.

Kneeling on the floor beside Amalia's bed was Karina, the source of the mumbling. When he took a step closer, he realized it wasn't mumbling, exactly. Karina was chanting in another language. His best guess was Latin, but he wasn't exactly sure.

He stood silently for a moment, listening. But then she stopped.

"You're very good at being quiet," Karina said, opening her eyes, "but I smelled you ever since you walked down the hall."

Shiro bit back a laugh. "This coming from someone who bathes in an actual swamp."

"We don't bathe in the swamp," Amalia said, grunting as she sat up. "We're no water mages, but we know how to boil water."

"Though magic does help it look less murky," Karina

added.

"What are you doing?" He gestured at the floor. "With the chanting, I mean."

Karina stood and stretched, exchanging a look with her grandmother. "Trying to do a magical detox. I don't know if whatever the dark mage did is a reversible kind of magic, but it's worth a try."

"Is it working?" Shiro asked.

Amalia tightened her jaw and grabbed the bedsheets, clenching them until her fingers turned red.

Shiro shifted from one foot to the other. "I'll take that as a no."

"I'm not giving up." Karina walked over to Amalia and rubbed her back. "I'll try some other herbs and… maybe a different spell. There's a full moon coming; I could try to harness the power of—"

"Karina, stop." Amalia covered her mouth to cough. "There's no use. That dark mage knew what he was doing. He wouldn't have done something to a witch that a spell would undo. That would be foolish."

"Maybe a spell isn't what is needed." Shiro scrubbed at his jaw.

Karina narrowed her eyes. "What do you have in

mind?"

"The plasma in human blood is ninety-two percent water. I'm assuming it's the same with swamp witches?"

"Yes." Karina smirked. "Except it's dirtier with possible tadpoles and dead mosquitos thrown in the mix."

Shiro felt his cheeks grow hot. "Sorry."

"What are you suggesting?" Amalia asked, cringing as she shifted on the bed.

"Well, it was your idea to do a detox." Shiro gave a half-shrug. "I'm just thinking of going a different route."

Karina stared at him a moment and then quickly turned toward her grandmother. "Manipulating the water in your blood? You think it would work?"

"It couldn't hurt," Amalia said.

"Actually… it might." Shiro cringed and came closer to the bed. "If I successfully extract poison from your body, it's going to have to come out somehow."

"Like…" Karina appeared as if she were holding back a wince. "She might throw it up?"

"That, or it could be pushed out through her pores. In any case, the poison is probably going to take a toll on whatever it comes into contact with."

Amalia took a deep breath and let it out slowly. With a nod, she leaned back until her head rested on her pillow. "Okay. Let's do it."

"Grandma, are you sure?"

"It's worth a try." Amalia closed her eyes. "I'm ready."

Karina swallowed hard, backing away from the bed.

Shiro wanted to tell her he would be careful, that he wouldn't let anything bad happen to her. But he couldn't promise that, and he didn't want to lie.

Amalia stretched out her fingers and blew out a breath. Her eyes were still closed, but she nodded once, giving Shiro the green light.

Shiro placed his palms together. He needed to take his time and do this right; otherwise, he could harm her heart or shatter her veins. For a moment, he had reservations about having mentioned his idea. If it didn't work, if he ended up killing Amalia, Karina would never forgive him. And he would never forgive himself.

He stretched out his arms, reaching toward Amalia until his fingers were mere inches away from her skin. The carnelian stone on his wristband caught the light. He felt outward with his power, tuning in to her blood. The current of her blood flow tingled in his fingertips.

He flinched, pulling his hands back for a second. Something hurt him. It was like splinters cutting through his skin. The farther he reached in, the sharper the pain. Sword tips. Razor blades. Hot, burning needles. Whatever magic the dark mage had used on her, it was killing her harshly.

Ever so gently, he pulled with his powers. Amalia let out a hiss, arching her back. Karina stepped forward quickly, worrying her hands, but she didn't approach the bed. Shiro carefully shifted his hand to the side. He could feel the poison crawl through her veins as he did so. Amalia clenched her teeth, but her moan of pain still escaped.

"Maybe we should stop," Karina said, her eyes darting between Shiro and her grandmother.

"No!" Amalia shook her head frantically. "Keep trying."

Shiro moved his hands horizontally, trying to separate the poison from Amalia's blood. He closed one hand into a fist and pulled it upward. Amalia let out a wail, grabbing at the sheets by her sides. Shiro pulled his power farther upward, his hands shaking.

"Shiro?" Karina scrubbed her hands down the sides

of her face.

"Just a little more," he said, his voice strained. He could feel the muscles in his neck tightening. He squeezed his fist tighter and yanked his arm upward.

Amalia gagged, rolled to her side, and vomited violently.

Shiro let go, his gaze flying to Karina as she ran to her grandmother's side. It wasn't until Amalia's second heave that Karina got the wastebasket under her head in time to catch her grandmother's sick.

A mixture of blood, yellow slime, and black particles landed in the wastebasket. It bubbled and sizzled, and it took all the control Shiro had not to throw up himself.

"Oh, Grandma," Karina cried, stoking her head.

Shiro wiped sweat from his brow and took a step back.

"Was that all of it?" Karina asked, her eyes brimming with tears.

"No." He took a deep breath and exhaled, shaking his head. "There's more. Lots more. But she's in a lot of pain. I think she should rest."

"No," Amalia said, her voice raspy. "Let's keep going."

"Amalia, the poison is strong. If I do too much at once, it'll rip your insides apart."

Karina's eyes grew wide. "He's right, Grandma. Let's take a break. Replenish your strength. We'll try again once you've rested."

Reluctance was etched on her face, but Amalia nodded. She rolled back onto the bed, trying to catch her breath. "All right. Just a little rest."

"I'll give you some space." Shiro turned to head out of the room, feeling as if his nerves were about to dissolve. Before he closed the door, he took one more glance at Amalia. She was breathing more steadily, but her face was pale, her eyes pinched closed.

Karina held her hand and looked up at Shiro. Her expression of sorrow and fear tore a hole in his soul.

Six

Penny inhaled, counting in her head. She tried to concentrate solely on her breathing, but she could literally feel Shiro's frustration. He sat in the lotus position, his eyes closed, attempting to meditate, but his frustration was palpable. She knew what he was trying to do, and she knew it was taking a toll on him.

She exhaled and then breathed in again. This time it was Yuki who distracted her. Her yoga moves were too fast, not at all graceful and fluid. She was more like a cheerleader practicing her jumping techniques.

"Why do we need to learn all this yoga anyway?" Kamal asked as he tried to copy her reverse warrior pose. "Seems silly."

She scowled at him. "So we can do things like this."

She was so fast, Penny almost couldn't track her movements. Yuki had swung her arms down to the mat and extended her right leg out in front of her. She swept it swiftly to the side, catching Kamal's leg and knocking him flat on his back.

Yuki smiled at Kamal's groan of pain. "Still seem silly to you?"

Penny pushed their conversation away and closed her eyes. For a while, a whirlwind of thoughts went through her mind. She ignored them, blocking them from her train of thought as she tried to draw a blank slate. After a while, her thoughts were clear, and she slowed her breathing.

A picture popped into her mind. The interior of some house, but seen through tunnel vision. Everything at the edges of the scene was blurred out. A fireplace. A pastel painting hanging above it. Someone walked by it, but she couldn't see who it was. In her vision, she followed them.

They went down the nearby hall and entered a dark room. They took a key out of their pocket and unlocked a door inside the room. The door led to what looked like a storage area, a large walk-in closet with shelves. And on the shelves were three red-and-black boxes. The daggers.

"All I'm saying is if I knew you were going to attack me, I would have been ready," Kamal said to Yuki.

Penny grunted in frustration. Even Shiro sighed with impatience.

"Can you two keep it down?" Penny asked.

Yuki and Kamal sheepishly apologized, and Penny closed her eyes again.

Come on, daggers. Show me where you are.

She cleared her mind once more. She searched for the vision, wanting to call it back so she could figure out where this place in her vision was.

Darkness. Shadows. Water.

Water?

She followed the thought. It was as if she were swimming through the water in her mind.

Bubbles. Fish. People looking through glass and pointing.

Penny's eyes flew open as she gasped.

"I found it," she said, jumping to her feet. "I know where the last dagger is."

There were still a few patrons at the aquarium. They had about fifteen minutes left before closing time, and the workers had already begun to rope off sections. Kamal used his sapphire-based charm to walk up to the straggling patrons, whispering to them. Loni watched them listen to him. Each person he approached seemed to nod in agreement with whatever he said and proceeded to leave. None of them noticed the blue glow of his palms, which he kept hidden behind his back.

Once the leftover patrons had gone, Kamal proceeded to get the workers to go. One of them removed their keys from their belt loop and handed them to him. Loni almost laughed at the extremes Kamal had gone to for this mission.

Once they were in the clear, Penny called them over. "Follow me."

They made their way down a tunnel that went

through the water. Fish swam above them and to their sides. At the end of the tunnel, the room opened up facing a gigantic wall of glass. Behind it loomed a wall of coral littered with sea anemones and flower-like clusters of pink polyps. Crown-of-thorns sea stars rounded the bases of the coral walls, and small mandarinfish swam around, searching for food. But what made Loni drop her jaw was the sand tiger sharks that loomed nearby.

"There are sharks in there," Loni whispered, as if they could hear her.

"There's also a dagger in there. An important one." Penny took her hands. "Shiro will help try to steer them away."

Loni looked up at Shiro.

"Yeah," he said. "I've, uh, only done it with smaller fish, but how different could it be?"

Loni fought off a shiver that crept up her back. "You're filling me with confidence, you know that?"

"Do you see that section of coral there?" Penny pointed, her finger on the glass. "Next to that blue starfish."

Loni drew closer to the glass and peered at the spot Penny spoke of. "Yeah."

"That seaweed should break away. The box is behind it."

Loni took a deep breath. "Okay. I can get it."

"You know what you're going to do?" Penny asked.

"I'll dive in and create an air bubble around my head so I can get low enough without having to come back up for air. But Shiro *has* to keep those sharks away."

"Guys," Kamal called. He waved them over to a door he'd unlocked. It read, "Staff Only."

They followed him through the door and made their way up a set of metal stairs. The stairs brought them to a platform that was suspended above all the tanks. The sound of the filters whirred in the air, and Loni could feel the vibration shaking her bones. Or maybe that was just her nerves.

They rounded the shark tank and Loni squatted down.

"Are you ready to do this?" Penny asked.

"As ready as I'll ever be," she answered.

Loni took off her shoes and swung her legs over the water. She winced as she dropped her feet inside. "Cold," was all she said.

Her palms glowed green, and she held them near her

ears. Instinct had her hold her breath as she jumped, but there was no need to do so. As soon as she was in the water, a bubble of air surrounded her head. She took a chance and breathed, hoping the bubble wouldn't pop. The green of her palms grew brighter, as she was determined not to lose her air bubble.

She looked up at Penny and the others, but they were blurry and wavering in her vision. It looked as though Kamal was giving her a thumbs-up. She turned her attention downward. The spot Penny told her about seemed so far away. She looked left and right, searching for where the sharks might be. She caught sight of one, but it was moving away from her.

It's now or never, she thought.

Loni shifted her position and kicked her feet, diving deeper into the water. Her eyes focused on the blue starfish. Panic threatened to do her in, but she forced it out of her mind. She had to get the dagger. This was their chance to get ahead of the Pishacha. Just a little bit farther.

A school of clownfish swam past her bubble as she reached for the seaweed Penny had told her to pull away from the coral. She muttered a curse directed at Shiro. He couldn't even keep the little fish away. But when she looked over her shoulder, she saw why. A tiger shark was twisting in the water, making its way toward her.

Loni gasped. Her feet kicked to back away from the shark, and her foot caught a sharp bit of coral. Holding back a yelp, she tried to keep from flailing. A small cloud of blood trailed away from the back of her foot.

No, no, no!

She stared wide-eyed at the approaching shark, afraid to move. The shark went left and right, jerking his head as if fighting off something causing resistance. Loni's breaths began to cloud the bubble. She fought back her panic and told herself to steady her breathing. The shark snapped its teeth in the water, aggravated by the unseen force that was keeping it from getting near Loni.

Thank you, Shiro, she thought.

Quickly, she turned and made her way back to the blue starfish and the seaweed. There was no telling how long Shiro could keep the shark away from her, and Loni knew there was at least one more in the tank. Her odds wouldn't improve if that one decided to join his friend.

The seaweed was slippery, but she managed to pull it away from the coral. Sure enough, there was a small section carved into the coral where the red-and-black box sat. It was wrapped in clear, tight plastic and tape. She pried the box out of the hole and held it against her chest.

Checking once more for the whereabouts of the sharks, she focused on the surface of the water and kicked her legs as hard as she could. Using a little more air power, she boosted herself to the surface. Her bubble popped as soon as she broke through.

Shiro and Penny pulled her out and set her on the platform. Kamal took the box. Even though she'd had air the entire time, she gasped as though she were breathing for the first time.

"You did great, Loni," Penny said.

"If I never see another shark for the rest of my life, it'll be too soon." Loni stood and wrung water out of her clothes. She grimaced at the murky grime that clung to her skin. "Let's get out of here. I need a shower."

Seven

Mayhara slipped her hands off Jae's waist and dismounted his bike. As she removed her helmet, she scanned their surroundings for Imperial Police and Pishacha. It was risky returning to the scroll shop, but they had the chance to find out more about the mysterious scroll they were in possession of. Even Penny wasn't able to give them insight on what the scroll was or why it was important.

The bell above the door chimed as they stepped into

the cluttered shop. The siblings Mayhara and Jae had met during their last visit to the shop looked up as they entered. Nian, the more cooperative and cordial of the siblings, packaged a purchase by a short, plump customer and wished her a nice day before nodding his greeting to Jae and Mayhara. Nian's sister, Zhen, simply raised a brow at them as she continued to dust a shelf of vases.

They were dressed similarly, Nian in a blue-and-black *tangzhuang* jacket and Zhen in a blue-and-black *cheongsam* dress. Nian's black hair was slicked back, while Zhen's thick, dark mane was pulled up and held in place with a matching blue *fa-zan* hairpin shaped in the form of a peacock.

Jae and Mayhara waited until the customer Nian had tended to was finished with her purchase. Mayhara pretended to inspect a carving of a dragon as the customer passed by her. For a second, the woman stopped. Mayhara's heart began to hammer in her throat. She calmly adjusted her turquoise headscarf and turned away from the woman. Forcing herself to breathe normally, Mayhara told herself the woman might just have been browsing the shelves once more before leaving. Finally, the woman continued walking. When the bell above the door signaled her departure, Mayhara let out a sigh of relief.

Nian walked around the counter and bowed to Jae. As Mayhara made her way over to them, Zhen scoffed and rolled her eyes. Mayhara shot her a questioning look, but Zhen ignored her and disappeared behind a curtain into what Mayhara assumed was the stockroom.

"Good to see you again." Nian bowed to Mayhara as she joined them.

"You too," she answered.

"Zhen is getting our great-aunt. I'll lock the door and close the shop temporarily so we can talk in private."

Jae nodded and glanced at Mayhara. She pushed back her headscarf and rocked onto her heels, fighting off a flutter in her stomach. Could this great-aunt of theirs really be able to solve the mystery of the cryptic scroll?

The curtain was pushed aside, and Zhen appeared, followed by a short, round-bodied, older woman with straw-like white hair and thick glasses. She hobbled behind Zhen as they approached the counter.

"This is our great-aunt Baozhai," Nian said.

"She can probably help you," Zhen said. "She's very old."

Nian scowled at Zhen and elbowed her hard.

"She's not wrong." Baozhai smirked. "She's also not in my will."

Zhen frowned and mumbled something in Mandarin.

"Thank you for offering to help." Jae bowed to her. "I realized there's a risk to working with mages, so we do appreciate it."

"Hmm. Don't thank me yet." She held out her hand. "Let's have a look first."

Jae and Mayhara exchanged a glance. Zhen and Nian watched them expectantly. Baozhai's hand was still out as she waited. Clearing his throat, Jae opened his messenger bag and withdrew the tube that held the scroll.

Baozhai took it, running her hand over the surface as if checking to see if it was authentic. She turned as she slipped the scroll out and then unrolled the delicate fabric on the counter. She used her fingers to smooth out the material. Adjusting her glasses, she leaned closer and studied the illustration.

Mayhara bit back her impatience. She desperately wanted to ask the woman what she saw but knew it was better not to interrupt her.

"First the bad news," Baozhai finally said. "I haven't seen this scroll before. It's from before my time. You can tell from the fabric that was used and the almost blueish tone of the ink."

Mayhara and Jae leaned closer to inspect the things she'd described.

"Since I haven't seen the scroll before," Baozhai continued, "I can't say with certainty I know what it is."

"Okay," Jae said. "I'm hoping there's some good news to counter that fact."

Baozhai squinted as she smiled at him. "There is. You see this symbol?" She pointed to a small square near the bottom of the scroll. The square had diagonal lines connecting the corners, forming an 'X' and a vertical line running through the middle of the square. "That's the symbol for *witch*. And this symbol next to it is an old language style of writing *book*."

"Witch book," Mayhara said to herself. "A grimoire?"

She and Jae exchanged a look. Amalia had mentioned a grimoire. Perhaps this was connected.

"And you think this is a map?" Jae asked Baozhai. "Nian mentioned the possibility."

"These twisting and turning lines"—Baozhai traced

the lines with her wrinkly finger—"to the common eye, they might appear to be the borders of land, but they could also represent the walls of a tunnel."

Mayhara put her hand on the corner of the scroll and adjusted her perspective. "Okay. But where is this?"

"I can't be sure." Baozhai shook her head. "But these symbols on the sides might be clues. Someone would have to decipher them."

"So basically, this scroll is a treasure map to a grimoire." Jae crossed his arms and pressed a thumb to his lips. Mayhara could almost see the wheels in his brain spinning.

"That's what it looks like." Baozhai rolled up the scroll and slipped it back in its tube. "I'm sorry I can't help you more. Most of those symbols are foreign to me, so unless you know where to find a witch—"

A hard banging on the door made them jump.

"Who is that?" Mayhara whispered.

"Imperial Police! Open up!"

Mayhara's hand shot out and grabbed Jae's arm. "Oh no. That woman who was in the shop. She must have recognized me and called the police."

Jae's head whipped around to face Nian. "Is there a

back way out of here?"

"Yes, follow me."

Mayhara's head swam as she and Jae rushed through the curtains into the back room. The police had found her. This could all go bad very fast. The room was jampacked with inventory, making it difficult to maneuver. There was a large door at the back of the room labeled WORKSHOP, but that wasn't where Nian led them.

Kicking a large box to the side, Nian grabbed a wall-high set of shelves and pried it away from the wall. Behind it was a hidden door.

"This way," he said, throwing the door open. "Keep going to the end of the hall. It comes out on the opposite side of the block into an alleyway. From there, you're on your own."

Mayhara nodded. She could hear Zhen telling the police the lock was stuck, asking for their patience.

"Thank you," Jae told Nian.

"Good luck," he replied.

He shut the door behind them, and they raced down the hall. Mayhara's jaw was set, and she flexed her hands, preparing herself to use her powers if necessary.

At the end of the hall, Jae yanked the door open. Mayhara squinted against the sun, adjusting her eyes to the change of light so she could better assess their escape route.

"Through here," Jae called, already at the gate of a chain-link fence dividing the alleyway.

Mayhara almost tripped over a crate blocking her way but managed to slip through the gate unscathed. They dashed to the end of the alleyway and pressed their backs against the wall of one building. Mayhara could hear the deafening sound of buzz saws through the workshop windows. Jae peered around the corner.

"Okay, let's go." Jae nodded to her once.

They only made it twenty feet before a loud voice boomed through the air.

"Imperial Police! Stop where you are!"

Mayhara made the mistake of looking over her shoulder at the officer who had shouted at them. In that instant, Jae had veered off to dive behind a dumpster, yelling for Mayhara to come with him. But that moment cost her a precious second of judgement. Another officer appeared in front of her, his gun drawn.

Mayhara's vision hazed over for a second. She could

hear one of the officers say "back up" and "fugitive" into his radio while the other commanded that she not move.

No. She had to concentrate.

A crimson glow came to life in each of her palms. The officer with the gun shouted at her to lower her hands. Instead, she forced out crimson energy on each side of her. The earth exploded between her and the Imperial Police, a barrage of debris kicking up and striking the officers, throwing them back. The officer with the gun trained on her fired his weapon, but the explosion had knocked him off balance, and the bullet missed.

Setting off another explosion, Mayhara crouched down and doubled back. She leaped to the spot Jae had gone and grabbed his arm. "Let's go!"

"This way," he said. "I can hear their backup coming from the other direction."

She didn't question him; she just ran. They didn't stop until they were two blocks down and had rounded the corner. As they paused to catch their breaths, Jae checked behind them.

"We've got a head start, but we can't stop."

She gaped at the blood on his jaw. "Oh my God, did I do that?"

"No, don't worry. I clipped it on the dumpster." He peered around the corner. "We can make it back to my bike if we cut through those buildings. You ready?"

She steeled herself and nodded. "Yeah, let's go."

Eight

It was peaceful in the garden. Naree watched a hummingbird flit around from flower to flower collecting nectar. It seemed tranquil, happy as it completed its task. Naree could almost forget the anguish she'd been in over the last few days at not completing her task.

Almost.

She stretched on the lounge chair and glanced through the sliding glass door. Seeing Bhutano come toward her, she sat upright and swung her legs off the leg rest to place her feet on the floor.

His short, dark hair was slicked back, his shoulders broad and squared. His heavy brows were drawn over his intense black eyes. His expression was pure business, yet the clenching of his jaw told Naree he had some bad news.

"Bhutano?" She had to clear her throat when his name hadn't come out right.

"Your majesty."

The fact that he called her this was already a good sign, in her mind. "Has something happened?"

"I've called a meeting with the council of the seven. They'll be arriving shortly, and you should attend."

"Of course," she said. "What's this about?"

"One of the elites had a run-in with the Imperial Police near a scroll shop in the city."

"A run-in?"

He nodded once. "They almost had her, but she managed to escape. Your... Your brother was with her."

Naree flinched. She wasn't sure what to think or how to feel. She'd been trained not to think of Jae as family. Naree was a reincarnation of Lakshmi, and Lakshmi had no brother.

Bhutano searched her face.

Maybe this is a test, Naree thought. *To make sure I'm still on Kashmeru's side.*

She cleared her throat, keeping her expression neutral. "A scroll shop? Does this have anything to do with the scrolls that were stolen from Censinq?"

"We believe so," Bhutano replied. "We're sending a team in to interrogate the shop staff."

Naree breathed in deeply and exhaled slowly. "And if they can't give us any answers?"

"Then our dark mages will have to step in and *make* them cooperate."

Nine

Mayhara and Jae split up as soon as they got to the temple. They'd agreed to divide their tasks. As Jae went to find Darshana and fill her in on the information they'd found out about the scroll, Mayhara headed off to find Amalia. She hadn't expected to find Karina in the hall, with her back pressed against her door. And she hadn't expected to find her crying.

"Karina! What—"

The sound of Amalia's strained moan from behind the door gave Mayhara pause.

Karina winced, wiping the tears from her cheeks.

"What's happening in there?" Mayhara whispered, placing a hand on Karina's shoulder.

"Shiro's trying to pull out the poison."

Mayhara's jaw hung open as she tried to process that. "He can do that?"

Karina shrugged. "It hurts her, though. I don't know what's worse: her suffering from the poison or from the extraction."

"Well, if it's working—"

"That's just it. He can only do it in short sessions without tearing apart her insides. Then, by the time she's rested enough for him to do more, he checks to see how much poison he can feel in her body, and it's multiplied. It's growing faster than he can remove it. He can't keep up with it, but neither one of them wants to give up."

Another moan of pain sounded from behind the door. Amalia's cry made Mayhara's heart tense up.

Karina drew her lips in, suppressing a sob. "I… I can't bear to watch or listen anymore."

Mayhara drew closer and put her arm around Karina.

She could practically feel Karina's worry seeping out of her pores. "Maybe you should take a walk, get some air."

Karina sniffled, nodding her head.

Mayhara took a step back and studied her face. "And if you're up for a distraction, I could really use your help with something."

"Sure." Karina fell into step with Mayhara as they made their way down the hall. "What is it?"

"We acquired a scroll that has something to do with the prophecy. Apparently, the symbols on it might be able to be interpreted by a witch. I was hoping you'd be able to take a look and see if you can translate any of it."

"Of course." Karina took her hand and squeezed it. "If it helps putting an end to Kashmeru's tyranny, count me in."

⟡

Jae leaned on the back of the couch, watching Darshana pace as she took in the information about the scroll. Mr. Kitaro and Penny, seated in the living room area, kept their eyes on her as well. Kamal, Loni, and Salina waited for her to speak, undoubtedly processing the news themselves.

"And Mayhara's asking Amalia to translate the symbols?" Darshana asked.

"Yes," Jae answered.

"Actually," Penny said, interrupting, "she asked Karina. They're out by the pond, looking over the scroll right now."

"How do you know that? You've been sitting here all…" Kamal scoffed. "Not going to lie. It's scary when you do that."

"Okay, so there's a chance we could figure out where the grimoire is." Salina raked her hands through the curls at her temples. "I mean, I know we said we were going to concentrate on getting the other daggers, but we've totally got to follow up on that, right?"

"Cover our bases." Mr. Kitaro nodded, coddling his coffee cup. "Yes, it's a strategic move."

"Should we really be deciding that yet?" Loni's tone was full of skepticism. "We don't even know if Karina can decipher the scroll, let alone figure out where The Archives are. We could be wasting our resources if we split up, especially if this turns out to be a wild goose chase."

"Have a bit more faith, Loni," Darshana said, finally standing still after pacing the entire room. "These things fall into our laps for reasons, especially when it comes to the prophecy. I don't think it's a coincidence that Amalia and Karina found their way to us in a time when needing a witch proves useful."

"Spooky," Kamal mumbled.

"We'll use our cognitive lessons from back at the academy," Salina said. "Make a plan."

"Yeah, between the group of us, we can come up with something that will work."

The back sliding door slid open. They all turned to see Mayhara and Karina stepping inside. Mayhara tapped the scroll tube against her palm.

"We've got something," Mayhara said.

Jae felt goosebumps spring up all over his skin.

"There are symbols at the bottom right of the scroll. Mayhara said she and Jae thought they might be Wiccan. But they're not Wiccan numbers. They're Bhahmi numerals."

"Numbers?" Jae asked. "Referencing what?"

"The way they're lined up," Mayhara began, "we

think they're coordinates."

Ten

A flash of color soared through the air toward Loni, and with it came an earsplitting, high-pitched tone that almost made her lose focus. Her palms glowed emerald green, and when she pushed out her mage powers, creating a blast of wind, the sound became muffled and distorted, and then disappeared. At the opposite end of the training field, Kamal smirked at her.

"Jerk," she mumbled.

The trill of laughter caught her ear. Loni followed the sound and spotted Mayhara on the far end of the field. Jae handed Mayhara a towel but playfully whipped it away before she could take it. Mayhara giggled and smacked Jae's bicep, her hand lingering there a second or two longer than Loni was comfortable with. Jae lifted the towel and hung it over Mayhara's shoulders.

Loni's insides grew hot, her breath like steam escaping from her nostrils. A part of her wanted to send a blast of emerald energy their way and knock Mayhara off her feet.

In that moment, Loni was pummeled into and slammed to the ground with force. It took her a minute before she realized it was Salina who'd collided with her.

Loni clenched her jaw and pushed Salina off her. "Watch it!" She rolled to the side and jumped to her feet.

Salina furrowed her brow as she regained her footing. "Sorry."

"My fault," Shiro called, running up to them. "That last ice blast was more powerful than I meant it to be."

"I didn't mean to crash into you," Salina said. "It's just that Darshana is pushing me extra hard now that I'm the golden elite, and keeping focus is—"

"I don't want to hear your excuses." Loni used her air powers to blow stray grass and leaves off her clothes. "It's always excuses with you. Maybe you should start taking responsibility for your actions for a change."

Salina scoffed. "What the hell is your problem?"

Loni was about to retort, but the other mages were approaching. Out of the corner of her eye, she spotted Darshana, watching them intently from the temple's terrace.

"Everything okay?" Jae asked.

"It's fine," Loni answered irately.

"A pity." Kamal rested his hands on his hips. "Thought we might get to see a catfight."

He began to meow, but Penny smacked him on the arm.

"Pig," Yuki mumbled.

A *ping* sounded, and Shiro took out his Linq. "Oh no."

"What is it?" Mayhara asked.

"There's been an attack on town hall," he answered.

The mages gathered closer, huddling over Shiro's shoulders to watch video footage a citizen had caught and uploaded to social media. The shaky video showed an explosion erupting through a section of windows on New Jaipur's town hall building. Passersby screamed as they fled.

The man holding the camera shouted, "I think a bomb just went off in the town hall! Smoke is filling the air. People are running away in case another bomb explodes. Who would do this?"

"Extremists?" Salina asked.

Kamal shrugged. "Who else could it be?"

Loni noticed Shiro's jaw tense as he put his Linq away.

"It was uploaded about half an hour ago," Yuki said as she pulled the elastic band out of her hair. "Let's go inside and see if any of it has made the news yet."

Loni took her time, trailing behind as the rest of the group headed inside to the living room televiewer. Her eyes followed Jae and Mayhara as they walked side by side. They weren't holding hands, nor did Jae have his arm draped around her shoulder. But there was a vibe between them that felt like a knife in Loni's gut. She knew she had no reason to feel territorial about him. She hadn't seen him in years.

They made it inside, followed by a curious Darshana

and Mr. Kitaro. Loni's thoughts were interrupted by the televiewer coming to life. Similar video footage to the one they'd seen on Shiro's Linq displayed on the screen.

"—that the involvement of extremists in the attack is just speculation at this point. However, the perpetrators seemed to have left a calling card of sorts, a symbol that denotes responsibility for the act. A small, black, plastic card with a gold skull and crossbones illustration was found at both the scene of the attack today as well as the incident at the Alwar police station last week."

The image on the screen changed from the burning town hall to a shot of the governor and his family being escorted into a limousine.

"Governor Laghari and his family were not physically harmed in the explosion, as they were in a different section of the building at the time for a press-related photoshoot, but they are scheduled to meet with a security specialist due to the upcoming costume gala in New Jaipur."

"Avi." Yuki's hands flew to her mouth.

"What?" Salina asked.

"The governor's son." Yuki visibly swallowed. "Avi. He's a dark mage."

"Are you sure?" Shiro asked.

"Yes," she said, dropping her gaze.

"Wait." Jae turned to the other mages. "That makes sense. The Sacred Key from the observatory—when she accused us of being dark mages, she asked which one of us was the governor's son."

"So it's true," Mayhara said.

"But how did you know?" Shiro asked Yuki.

Yuki pursed her lips.

"They used to be a couple," Kamal said.

"Not a couple." Yuki smacked his shoulder and crossed her arms. "We went on, like, two dates. But this was before I found out he was a dark mage. As soon as I found out, I cut ties with him—which he wasn't too happy about. So I used my emotion powers to convince him he was fine with the break."

"Wait. Dates?" Salina asked. "Aren't you fourteen?"

Yuki narrowed her eyes at her. "I'm seventeen."

"Penny?" Mayhara asked.

Everyone turned to see Penny holding the controller,

which was pointed at the televiewer. The screen was frozen on the interior of a building. Loni realized it was the building the gala would take place in. The shot zeroed in on a fireplace. Two tall cast-iron candle holders stood on either side. Above it was a painting of a girl smelling a lotus.

"Penny, what is it?" Loni asked.

"I've seen this before. This fireplace, the painting. I've seen them in my visions." Penny turned to the others. "I think I know where the Pishacha are hiding the daggers."

Everyone's eyes went to the screen.

"At the governor's mansion?" Jae asked.

"We've got to go get them." Kamal stood, puffing out his chest as if ready to go.

"Don't be so hasty." Darshana, who had been quietly watching them for some time, stepped closer. "They will have armed guards at all times of the day and night. Especially now, with the recent attacks. No one will be able to get close to that place."

"But they will on the night of the gala," Yuki said.

"Only prominent people." Loni swiped her hair out of her face. "I believe it's invitation-only."

"So we get invited," Jae said.

"What?" Mayhara shook her head. "How's that supposed to happen?"

"It shouldn't be hard for a sapphire mage to convince whoever is at the door that they belong there." Jae looked pointedly at Kamal. "It's a costume ball. Everyone will be wearing masks."

"It could work," Mr. Kitaro said, also stepping forward from the back of the room. "If we got someone in, they might be able to get to the daggers."

"Sure," Kamal said. "I can do that."

"You shouldn't go alone," Penny said. "This isn't a solo job. Plus, you'd have a better chance at not raising suspicions if you had a date. Not me, though. I need to go into vision-mode to figure out where the daggers are, and people might notice."

"I'll do it," Loni said. "I love masks."

"I can get some devices so Penny can communicate with you over an earpiece," Jae added. "A couple of us can be near but out of sight to make sure we've got a clean escape route."

"Okay, it's settled," Darshana said. "And while we await the gala, we can try to figure out how to find the grimoire."

A warm, comforting feeling filled Jae's heart when Mayhara opened her door and smiled at him. He'd been rehearsing in his head what he wanted to say to her, but now, gazing into her deep brown eyes, he was at a loss for words.

"Jae?"

"I wanted to… Is it okay if I come in and talk to you?"

"Of course." She opened the door wider and stepped aside.

Her bedsheets were slightly pulled back. Jae wondered if she had been lying down, and for a moment he felt bad for disturbing her. But he'd been driven here by a force he couldn't ignore, so instead of apologizing, he decided to open up.

"Mayha, maybe this is going to sound ridiculous, but I can't get it out of my head. I tried to play it off all day, as if it hadn't affected me, but I just can't shake it."

"What is it?"

He cleared his throat. "Yesterday, when you almost

got caught… I… I thought my heart was going to stop."

"It's not ridiculous." She offered him a small smile. "I'm pretty sure mine did. At least, for a few seconds."

"I don't know what I would have done if they'd taken you away." He let out the smallest of laughs. "I mean, I do. I would have done anything in my power to get you away from them. But one of them took a shot at you. The panic that brewed up inside me… I could feel it in my throat."

She reached up and ran a finger along the laceration on his jaw. "Looks like you actually got the worst of it."

He trapped her hand with his, holding it to his cheek. "It's just a scratch. Especially compared to how my fear for your life tore a gaping hole in my heart."

She searched his face, her lips parting. Her thumb caressed her cheekbone, and she took a step closer.

Jae let his face hover nearer to hers, his eyes taking in every tiny movement of this moment, the way her lids grew heavy, the soft brush of her breath against his skin. Slowly, he closed the distance between them. There was no second-guessing now. The moment he'd been dreaming of had come to fruition.

Her lips were soft and warm, and as she drew in a

breath—the kiss along with it—she pressed her chest against him. Jae cupped his hands around the back of her head, like he was afraid the kiss would end too soon.

Before his heart could explode, he moved his lips to her cheek, her temple, her forehead, and then he pulled her into a crushing embrace. Her hands traveled up and down his back as he stroked the back of her head. He wasn't sure if the hammering in his chest was coming from her heart or his.

"I was afraid," she whispered, "to let myself believe you could feel this way about me."

"You never have to be afraid with me. We're in this together, remember? You're stuck with me for a while."

"For a while?" She chuckled.

"Forever," he said. "Or until the end of the world. Whichever comes last."

She laughed softly as she drew back. He took her hands and gazed at her a moment longer.

"I should let you get some sleep." He let go of her hands and raked his fingers through his hair. "To be honest, today has left me exhausted."

"Me too." She gave him a warm smile. "I'll see you in the morning."

He reached out and trailed his thumb down her cheek. "Good night."

He left the room with the feeling he was floating. His heart thrummed with exhilaration and his breaths came easy. It was as if he'd just removed a layer of armor. He had to stop himself from skipping to his room like a kid. If anyone were to see him, they'd think he'd already singlehandedly won the war.

But someone did see him.

At the end of the hall, standing with her hand on her doorknob, was Loni.

Jae's smile faded as he walked past her. His stomach felt heavy when their eyes met for a split second. The look she gave him was filled with mixed emotions he couldn't quite interpret. He didn't even want to guess what she was thinking.

He forced himself to look away, continuing to his room. He didn't have time to deal with Loni right now. He was too exhausted. And he wasn't about to let her rain on his parade.

Eleven

Mayhara turned over in her bed for the hundredth time. But this time it wasn't dark mages and approaching comets keeping her up. Though she felt a little guilty for dwelling on it under such dire circumstances, she couldn't get the kiss with Jae out of her head. It wasn't that she hadn't wanted it to happen, and it wasn't that she regretted it. But she couldn't shake the twinge of guilt lurking in her bones for finding a hint of happiness while others were imprisoned and getting killed.

She punched her pillow with a grunt and then threw her covers off her body. Sighing, she sat up and swung her legs off the bed. Maybe a tea would help settle her nerves.

When she got to the kitchen, she found Kamal sitting in the breakfast nook, scarfing down leftovers.

"Don't mind me," he said between bites. "I'm always hungry."

"I noticed." She opened a cabinet and took out a tea cup.

"Can't sleep?" he asked.

She filled a kettle and set it on the stove. "Can't shut off my brain."

"Maybe a plate of *chana aloo* would help."

"I'm fine with green tea. Thanks."

She could feel him watching her as she prepared her hot drink. She wanted to ignore him, but it finally got to her.

"What?" There was no malice in her voice. Just exhaustion. She walked over with her tea and sat across from him at the table.

"Is it your family?"

"Is what my family?"

"The reason you can't sleep."

She tried to hide the blush that blossomed in her cheeks by taking a sip of her tea. If she wanted to share her feelings about Jae with someone, Kamal wasn't exactly the first person she'd seek out. "One of the reasons," she said. "What about you?"

"Oh, I don't have a family. Not a real one anyway."

"What does that mean?"

Kamal set his fork down and wiped his mouth with a cloth napkin. "It means my mom abandoned me when I was a baby. No idea who my dad is. Spent my youth bouncing from one foster home to another. The closest I'd come to calling someone family was Sunan."

"The sapphire elite at the time of the Eradication," she noted.

"Yeah. And obviously, he's not around anymore— nor are the other sapphire elites ahead of me. Otherwise, I wouldn't be here."

Mayhara toyed with the handle of her cup. "I'm sorry. I didn't know your history. It sounds rough."

"Kind of falls into the shadows. You know, with the possible end of the world coming about. But yeah."

A noise in the corridor cut into their conversation. Kamal raised his brows, his eyes locked with Mayhara's. Her brows, however, went in the opposite direction. She tried to ask him what the source of the sound might be without speaking, but he only shrugged. He didn't seem interested, but Mayhara was too curious. Besides, they had enemies out there. She had to make sure no one had broken in with the purpose of murdering them all.

Keeping light on her feet, Mayhara slipped out of the breakfast nook and headed toward the corridor, her hands stretched and ready, just in case. Peering into the darkness, she spotted Loni slipping on a leather jacket.

"Loni?" Mayhara whispered.

Loni froze for a second but averted her gaze when she realized it was Mayhara who'd called her name.

"Where are you going?" Mayhara asked.

Loni set her jaw, her mouth in a straight line. She narrowed her eyes at Mayhara. "Out."

Without another word, Loni whipped around and charged out the door. For a moment, Mayhara stood there, dumbfounded. When she sobered and went back into the kitchen, Kamal was still eating, seemingly disinterested in what had taken place in the hall.

"That was Loni," Mayhara said, still puzzled by the encounter. "She just… left. Said she was going 'out.'"

Kamal nodded as he finished chewing. "Yeah. She does that."

Mayhara blinked. "What do you mean?"

"Granted, I've only been pulled into this group recently. But I've noticed it enough. She disappears when she's upset about something."

"I mean, we're all upset. But running out in the middle of the night is reckless."

"I don't think she's upset about the same thing you are." Kamal pointed his fork at her.

"What makes you say that?"

"Because I know something I'm guessing you don't."

Mayhara scoffed. "What are we, eight? Just tell me." She lifted her tea, slowly sipping.

Kamal licked his fork and placed it on his empty plate. "Fine. I think Loni's having a hard time seeing you and Jae together because they used to be a thing."

Mayhara choked on her tea, coughing and spurting as she tried to catch her breath. "Wait. What?"

Kamal smirked. "See. You didn't know."

"First of all, what makes you think Jae and I are

together?"

"Oh, okay." He raised a brow. "That's how you want to play it."

Mayhara was about to object, but she knew if she did, Kamal might not tell her about Jae's past relationship with Loni. And she really needed to know.

"Fine." Mayhara checked the doorway, listening to make sure no one was coming. "We might have… a connection. But it's not like we've had a chance to define it or even talk about old flings."

She waited, but Kamal just shrugged and brought his plate to the sink.

"So, they were a thing?" she finally asked. "Back at the academy?" She tried to remember seeing them together, but it wasn't something that stuck out in her mind.

"No. After the Eradication."

"After?" Her face felt hot, and her heart began to speed up. "How?"

"From what she told me, Jae rescued her. They escaped together when the government tore up the school."

Mayhara felt a heaviness in her stomach. She placed

a hand on her throat, finding it a little hard to breathe. "What happened? I mean, why aren't they together anymore?"

"I don't know." Kamal stuck his hands in his pockets. "You should ask Jae."

She felt as if she'd been separated from her body, looking down on herself, unable to move. Kamal watched her for a second, his eyes flitting around her face.

"Yeah," she finally said. "I probably will. But, um, do me a favor? Don't say anything to him. Or to Loni. About this conversation, I mean. I just need to wrap my head around it a bit more before I bring it up with him."

"Sure thing." He gave her a wink and headed out of the kitchen. "Good luck."

Twelve

Rain made the streets glisten under the light of the moon. The streetlamps were reflected in the puddles Loni passed as she navigated through downtown New Jaipur. She knew this area was far from safe. She knew because she'd been here before on more than one occasion. And her reasons for being here hadn't exactly been honorable.

Ignoring the sweat beading along her hairline, she concentrated on keeping alert as she passed a group of homeless people. They were gathered around a trash can, a blazing fire inside it warming their hands. One of them—a man with a dirty beard—watched her closely. She pretended not to notice. When he took a step toward her, she used her emerald powers to feed the fire with a burst of air. The fire roared as the flames shot upward, bright embers kicking up into the air. The group, including the man who had been watching her, flinched from the sudden change. Loni kept her head down and continued down the street.

Checking the street signs, she noted she was two blocks away from her destination. She knew she shouldn't have been going there, and she knew this course of action was one of self-destruction, but she couldn't stop herself. She needed a fix. And she needed it now.

When she reached the alleyway, she looked down and adjusted her jacket. Her body was shaking, but she couldn't tell if it was because of the cold wind the rain had brought or because of the anxiety that had crept into her veins.

A sense of relief overcame her when she spotted the familiar face, but it was short-lived when she remembered he'd denied her his services the last time she'd gone to him.

Li Jun sat on the back steps to a long-abandoned restaurant kitchen, the place that was now what he liked to call his laboratory. His head was shaved, allowing the large tattoo over his left ear to be visible, and there was an intentional cut in one of his eyebrows. His army-green trench coat clung to his muscles as he ran his knife along a sharpening stone. The sound grated Loni's nerves.

She inhaled deeply and let out a long breath when his eyes met hers. Rubbing the back of her damp neck, she approached him. His second-in-command—Nadia, Loni remembered—stepped between them and glared at her with her light gray eyes. A tiny blue jewel piercing jutted out over the right side of her mouth.

"How dare you show your face here again." Nadia clenched her teeth.

"Nadia, let her approach."

"But, Li Jun, last time—"

"I have a feeling Loni wants to apologize for last time. Isn't that right, Loni?" Li Jun raised a brow as he waited for her to answer.

Nadia swept her short, pink bob behind her ears and stepped aside so Loni could approach.

"Well?" Li Jun kept his eyes on Loni as his blade slid against the stone. "What's it going to be?"

Loni desperately wanted to cross her arms to stop herself from shaking, but she didn't want to seem weak. Weakness in this part of town could mean death.

"Look, Li Jun. I'm sorry about trying to scam you last time. I was... I wasn't thinking clearly. It was the *Moxy* controlling me."

"If I were to forgive you, what's to stop you from trying to pull that crap off again?"

She averted her gaze. "The scar Nadia left on my body is a solid reminder not to repeat my mistakes."

Nadia rested her hands on her hips and smirked.

"So I assume you didn't come here just to apologize." Li Jun smiled, but it didn't reach his eyes.

"No. I need a hookup." Loni's voice was small.

"It's been a while," Li Jun said. "I thought maybe you decided to get clean."

"I wanted to." Loni's head filled with visions of her sister screaming for help. She ran a hand over her face to stop the memory. "Look, are you going to sell to me or not?"

"You've got credits?" Li Jun asked.

Loni pulled out her Linq. "I've got eighty-two."

He sucked at his teeth. "That'll get you a hundred milligrams."

Loni's brow wrinkled. "That's it?"

"What can I say?" Li Jun shrugged. "Inflation."

"That's like two pills. That's not going to last very long."

"Well, you got something else to bargain with?" Li Jun inspected his knife.

"She's got a shiny jewel on that bracelet of hers," Nadia said.

Loni put a hand over her emerald. Part of her wanted to rip if off and hand it over, trade the stone for double the Moxy. But deep down, she knew she'd need its power to keep her alive when the time came to fight the Pishacha.

"No." She stuffed her hands in her pockets. "I can't trade it."

Nadia stepped forward. "Now I'm even more interested in it."

"I said it's not an option. I'll just take the hundred for now."

"Come on, Loni." Li Jun tilted his head. "Throw in

the wristband and I'll make it three hundred milligrams."

She stiffened, gritting her teeth. Her mind volleyed her choices, and her stomach clenched with unease. She couldn't risk it, no matter how much she needed the Moxy. She was the elite emerald mage. She needed to keep her wristband.

"Not this time," she said, trying to throw them off.

"Fine." Li Jun tucked his knife away. "Transfer the credits."

Loni pulled out her Linq and tapped a few buttons on the screen. She then extended the end of the Linq toward Nadia. Once Nadia touched her Linq to Loni's, a *bleep* sounded, notifying them that the transfer was complete. Li Jun dangled a tiny, sealed plastic bag between two fingers. Loni swallowed hard as she reached out and took the bag.

"Pleasure doing business with you, Loni," Li Jun said, his tone sarcastic.

"See you soon." Nadia chuckled.

Loni kept her pace steady as she turned away from them and left the alleyway. She cursed her body for continually shaking. All she could think about were the pills in her pocket.

As she reached the street, a siren blared. Red and blue flashing lights illuminated the surroundings as the Imperial Police car raced in her direction. Loni held her breath, turning away from the car and ducking her head. She breathed in deeply through her nose and exhaled slowly, attempting to calm her thrashing heart. Closing her eyes, she listened as the siren grew closer. Then, in a dizzying moment, the tone of the siren changed. The car passed, continuing its race down the street.

As the blare of the siren faded, Loni pushed down the nausea that threatened to bring up her dinner. Her fingers closed around the bag of pills in her pocket. The Moxy called to her, promising to dull her grief and give her an escape from her sorrow.

She couldn't wait until she got back to the temple. She needed her fix now. It was only two pills, enough for one hit. But maybe this could be the last time she'd need a fix. She'd quit after this. One last fix of Moxy, and then she'd be done.

Checking over her shoulders, she ducked into an abandoned shop whose door stood slightly ajar. The streetlights lit up the windows. The shop was mostly empty except for a counter and shelves covered in blankets of dust.

Loni pressed her back against the wall near the door and pulled the bag of pills out of her pocket. Fingers shaking uncontrollably, she grasped the small, round, white pills. Her breaths came fast and heavy as she stared at them. This was wrong, she knew it. This was not behavior becoming of an elite mage. But it was the only way to stop the ache in her heart. And she was going to quit anyway, wasn't she?

She shoved the pills in her mouth and closed her eyes, letting the plastic bag drop away. Her eyes still shut, she slid down the wall until she was sitting on the floor.

Images of her sister, Kanya, filled her mind. Tears spilled down her cheeks as she thought about her sister's smile, her laugh, her embrace.

Kanya was dead, and Loni hadn't even tried to save her.

Guilt pressed in on her chest, threatening to suffocate her. Sobbing, she pulled her knees closer. Her grasp on her legs was so tight, she thought she might tear holes in her jeans.

The memory of the last time she saw Kanya played out in her head.

It sounded like fireworks were exploding around them. Smoke filled the air, and the ground shook. Loni ran to the window, looking down at the courtyard, and spotted her sister scrambling for cover with the rest of the students outside.

"Kanya!" Loni banged on the glass, but Kanya didn't hear her.

Loni's breath hitched. She ran from the dorm room to the stairwell. Screams echoed all around her. Loni didn't know what was making the building shake, but it was causing her head to throb as she bounded down the stairs.

Using her air power, she skipped the last few steps, landing on the main floor with a thud. When she reached the door to the courtyard, a blast of fire and debris threw her back. Her head caught the marble column in the hall. Everything went black. She couldn't move. Sounds faded in and out.

Someone grabbed her from under her arms and dragged her. She wanted to shout to the person to leave her alone. She didn't want these intruders to take her away. She needed to get to her sister. But even opening her mouth to speak sent shockwaves of pain shooting into her brain. The ache was too much. She felt herself slipping in and out of consciousness.

Another explosion went off somewhere in the school.

She opened her eyes to find that the person who'd dragged her from the hall was a boy she only slightly remembered seeing around the academy.

"What's happening?" she asked him, barely able to pronounce the words.

"It's the Imperial Police. The government has approved the Eradication proposal. They're abolishing the academy."

"Oh my God!" She sat up, her head spinning. "Kanya!"

She ignored the boy's protests as she charged for the hole in the wall where the door used to be. Smoke and flying debris blocked her vision. She threw out her emerald powers to clear the way so she could find her sister.

At the far end of the courtyard, Kanya was being forced into electro-cuffs by Imperial Police.

"Kanya!"

"What are you doing?" The boy grabbed her, sounding scared.

"That's my sister." She shook off his hand. "Kanya!"

Kanya whipped her head around and found Loni. Her eyes were wide with fear and tears stained her cheeks. Her temple was bruised and bleeding, and the sleeve of her blouse *was torn.*

"Loni!" Kanya flailed away from the police officer who was cuffing her, attempting to run to her sister. But she was suddenly struck with a long glowing baton that crackled with electricity as it made contact with her neck. Kanya fell to the ground, her fingers reaching toward Loni.

Loni screamed. She tensed her muscles, ready to run toward her sister, but the boy grabbed her arms and pulled her back just as another explosion went off close by.

"No. Don't go out there. You'll be killed." He was stronger than she'd guessed. "Come with me. I know a place to hide."

Loni almost gagged as the Imperial Police struck Kanya again. This time, Kanya didn't move.

"I need to save my sister," Loni yelled at the boy, her voice cracking with her sobs.

His hold on her was firm as he peered through the chaos. "She's already dead. I'm sorry. We can make it out alive, but you need to follow me."

Her breaths were drowned by her sobbing as she let him pull her along. Her mind swirled with fear, sorrow, anger, and confusion. What was happening? How had it come to this?

And Kanya… Kanya was dead.

The next thing she knew, the boy was leading her down stone steps. The went through a long corridor that eventually led to a double door made of withering wood. The boy pulled her inside.

Loni looked around, her vision clouded by her tears. "Is this a cave?"

"I guess you could call it that," he answered.

They were surrounded by stone, but the center of the room had a dropped bottom, and a large column of lights stood, reaching from the cavern floor far below up to the rock ceiling above them. It was a spiral edifice split into seven sections. Each section was divided by glowing particles of different colored elements: red at the bottom, swirling upward through orange, yellow, green, blue, and purple, then ending at the top with a brilliant white.

Loni wiped the tears from her face, but her body still shook. "What is this place?"

"We're under the school. I think this has something to do with the Lotus." He looked back at the door. "But I don't think anyone knows about this place. They shouldn't be able to find us here. We can wait until the attack is over. Until they leave. When it's clear, we can escape. I know a place we

can lie low."

Loni sniffled. "Why are you helping me?"

"I'd help more if I could, but the attack was so fast, and you were the only one nearby."

She was quiet for a moment, staring at the column of magical lights.

"Thank you," she finally said. "My name is Loni, by the way."

"Nice to meet you, Loni. I'm Jae."

The sound of glass breaking stirred Loni from the memory. Her head spun as she jumped to her feet. Though her face and fingers and skin felt numb from the Moxy, her brain was scrambling to be on high alert.

It might have just been a rat that had made the noise. But she couldn't be sure.

She steadied her balance and scanned the store. Adjusting her eyes to the dark, she spotted two figures moving toward her from a back room.

Gasping, she raised her hands between herself and the strangers. The room seemed to tip to the side as her vision doubled. Were there really four strangers now? She squeezed her eyes shut and shook her head, quickly opening them again.

No. Only two.

But she was intoxicated, and her reflexes were off. She had to get out of there. Whether they were Pishacha or ordinary street thugs, she didn't have the time or the opportunity to figure it out.

Steeling herself, she bolted for the door.

"Get her!" one of them said as they raced after her.

The cold, damp air helped to partially clear her mind. But still, she was unsure she could fight off her pursuers. Her shoes splashed through puddles as she ran. She knew she was heading in the wrong direction, what with the sub-train station east instead of west, but she couldn't stop now. The strangers weren't far behind. She'd have to try to lose them and double back.

With a quick glance over her shoulder, she made a move. Her palms glowed green as she cast out her power. The manhole in the street was blasted upward by air, hitting one of her pursuers hard in the face. Loni only looked back long enough to see he was knocked out—or possibly dead.

One down.

She turned the corner, nearly losing her balance. She

could barely catch her breath, but she couldn't afford to slow down. Her crucial mistake was veering into an alleyway that stopped in a dead end.

Muttering a curse, she raised her chin and looked upward. With her powers at full capacity, she might have been able to generate enough air to lift her to one of the rooftops. But the buildings swayed in her vision. The numbness taking over her skin had reached deeper inside her, making her muscles limp. There was no way she'd make the jump. Not like this.

She'd picked a fine time to indulge her addiction. If she had just waited until she'd gotten back to the temple—

The other man appeared in the alleyway, blocking her only exit. Loni's breaths were frantic as panic began to set in.

"What do you want?" she yelled.

The tall, lanky man came closer, ignoring her question. She could just make out the sneer on his face.

"Stay away from me!" She squared her shoulders, despite her urge to shrink into herself and disappear.

Still, he neared.

She couldn't stop the whimper that escaped her

mouth. Her instincts took over, and she raised her palms in his direction. One second, he was smirking, clearly reveling in his victory of having trapped his victim. The next second, the man froze, his eyes practically popping out of his head and his jaw hanging open. He grabbed his neck, his face drained of color as choking sounds erupted from his throat.

Loni's breaths were gasps as she kept her powers trained on him and gave him a wide berth, moving past him. He shot one hand out to reach for her, but she backed away, concentrating on keeping the air out of his lungs. And when he dropped to his knees, Loni turned and ran as fast as she could.

Thirteen

The cup of coffee warmed Mayhara's hand. She held it close as she entered the office where Jae was working. It was almost symbolic. Like she was keeping something familiar and comforting between her and Jae. She was trying to get her nerve up to ask him about his alleged past relationship with Loni, but she was going to need a lot more than coffee to give her courage.

On the other hand, she couldn't even be sure Kamal had been telling the truth about the relationship. It was one of the sapphire powers, after all: Making people believe lies.

"Good morning." She slipped into the chair across from Jae, despite her temptation to lean into him and give him a kiss.

He stopped typing and looked up at her. His smile seemed to cover his entire face. "Morning. How did you sleep?"

"Great." She hoped he wasn't using his powers to detect her fib. She needed to shift the focus off of her. "What about you? It looks like you've been up for a while."

"Karina translated the coordinates from the scroll, so I plugged them in. They point to the Bhaja Caves in Pune."

"Pune? That's like twenty hours from here."

"If there's no traffic, yeah. So I'm trying to get as much intel as I can before we plan a trip out there."

"We?" A blush crept up her face.

He grinned. "Are you up for it?"

"Sure." She squeezed her coffee cup, fighting off the butterflies in her stomach.

"We need to wait for Karina to finish interpreting the

rest of the symbols on the scroll first. But if we want to get our hands on the grimoire before the Pishacha do, we need to be sure we know where to look."

She nodded. It wasn't that she wasn't paying attention to him, but she couldn't stop staring at his lips.

Noticing her gaze, Jae leaned forward on the desk. "You okay?" he whispered. His grin wasn't as wide as before, but it was still there.

The question she'd been dying to ask him all morning danced in her mind.

I should just ask him.

She opened her mouth to speak, still not sure exactly what she was going to say, but Shiro walked into the room. She lifted her coffee and took a sip.

Jae and Mayhara both sat back in their seats, widening the distance between them.

"How's it going, Shiro?" Mayhara asked. "Any progress with Amalia?"

Shiro scrubbed his hands down his face, the dark circles under his eyes a stark contrast to his color-drained face. "You want the sugar-coated version, or do you want the truth?"

Mayhara grimaced. "That bad?"

"I thought the syphoning was working," Jae said.

"Yes and no." Shiro raised his arms above his head to stretch. When he lowered them, he released a sigh filled with exhaustion. "I can only get so much poison out without ripping her apart. And then the problem is that any poison left inside her multiplies until it fills her again."

Mayhara had no response. She realized that deep inside her, she had believed Shiro's plan would work. She had held on to the hope that together they could accomplish anything. Now, suddenly, a seed of doubt was planted, and she feared it might sprout and spread and destroy any optimism she had that they could win this war.

"Way to bring down the room, right?" Shiro leaned forward and picked up a paper from the desk. "What's this?"

"That," Jae said, pointing to the paper with a pen, "is the blueprint to the governor's mansion. Penny took a look at it and said she couldn't see any room that matched what she saw in her vision, so we're going on location."

"How are we getting in?" Shiro asked.

"They've started preparations for the gala." Jae

shrugged. "Kamal and I can use our powers to convince them we're part of the staff."

"As long as there's no Pishacha around," Mayhara added.

"If there are, we'll lie low," Jae said. "But at the very least, we can get a lay of the land, figure out escape routes and weak spots."

"Yeah." Shiro nodded. "Sounds good. Count me in."

"Are you sure?" Mayhara shook her head. "No offense, but you look like crap. Don't you want to get some sleep?"

"I don't think I could if I wanted to," Shiro replied. "My mind would just be running circles around this puzzle with Amalia. Might do me some good to get out and concentrate on something else for a bit."

"All right." Jae gave him a curt nod. "It's a plan."

"What's that one?" Shiro pointed to another set of blueprints.

Jae pushed the paper closer to Shiro. "This one is a blueprint of the Bhaja Caves. It's where the coordinates encrypted in the scroll point to, so we're betting the grimoire is hidden somewhere inside. Between that and the website's virtual tour videos, I can't seem to find anything that might lead to a space that matches the illustration on the scroll."

"Karina's still interpreting the other symbols on the scroll," Mayhara said. "So hopefully it'll give us more insight."

Shiro studied the blueprint. "The Bhaja Caves."

"Have you ever been to them?" Mayhara asked.

"When I was a kid." Shiro gave them a half-shrug. "The memory is kind of a blur."

Jae shifted in his chair. "So you wouldn't remember if there was some blocked-off section, maybe restricted access or construction or something?"

"No." Shiro raised a brow. "But I bet we'll find it if we know where to look."

✿

The day had grown hot. Or maybe it was just Shiro's exhaustion catching up with him. He pulled at the collar of his T-shirt, attempting to get some air to cool off his sweat-covered skin. He desperately wanted to remove the cap from his head, but he couldn't take the risk. The cap and sunglasses weren't the best of disguises but were necessary to keep from being recognized.

Kama's voice came to him over the earpiece. "Heading to the south entrance."

Shiro resisted touching the device in his ear. It would look too suspicious. "Watch out for the gazebo. There's a handful of Imperial Police headed that way."

"Copy that," Kamal answered.

"I'm going to try to slip in with the decorating staff," Jae announced.

"I'm keeping an eye on the north entrance." Yuki's voice was small and reflective of her age.

"Just make sure you're keeping your distance," Jae said. "We don't want that ex-boyfriend of yours spotting you."

"He's not my ex-boyfriend," Yuki said. "We only saw each other a couple times."

"Still, keep out of sight." The earpiece clicked as Jae signed off.

Yuki wasn't supposed to be scoping out the location with them. Since Loni would be attending the gala with Kamal, it made sense for her to become as familiar with the governor's mansion as possible. But apparently Loni had told Darshana she wasn't feeling well and stayed in bed. Penny was back at the temple meditating with Darshana about the dagger location, Salina was keeping an eye on Amalia, and Mayhara was taking notes with Karina as they tried to break the code in the scroll.

Yuki wore sunglasses, and a dark blue headscarf covered her auburn hair. As long as she kept herself inconspicuous, there shouldn't be a problem.

Shiro pretended to be a tourist photographing the city as he snapped pictures of the windows, the staff entrances, and the stations of security personnel. There was no doubt security would be at least doubled for the gala, but the mages would have a basis to build on.

The lavish two-story mansion stood regally behind an eight-foot cast-iron fence. Terracotta columns lined the building on three sides. The circular driveway at the front was adorned with ancient banya trees. Trucks were parked along the service entrance side, with hired help setting up tents and carrying in rented tables and festive decorations for the upcoming gala.

"Uh, guys," Kamal said. "We've got a problem."

"I hear it." Jae muttered a curse.

Shiro lowered the camera and glanced around. He

couldn't hear anything, but he didn't have the advantage of having sapphire powers.

"This doesn't feel good," Yuki said. It sounded as if she were running. "There's a lot of anger and hostility coming this way."

"Pishacha?" Shiro asked.

"I don't know," Yuki answered. "But it's big."

The hairs on Shiro's neck stood at end. Part of Yuki's diamond mage powers was emotion, Shiro noted. And if she was panicking about a force of anger and hostility heading toward them, then he was going to follow her lead.

He turned and hurried in her direction but froze in place suddenly when gunfire ripped through the air. Screams erupted around him. Women grabbed their children and ducked low to the ground. Others darted behind shops and stands to take cover.

He heard the shouts and chants of protest then.

Extremists.

More gunshots sounded.

A little girl, standing alone by a fountain, released the balloon she'd been holding and began to cry. Her mother, who hid behind a bench holding a baby, called out to her.

It was apparent she didn't want to expose the baby but desperately wanted her child to come to her.

Shiro ran to the child and swooped her up in one quick movement. In a matter of seconds, he placed the girl at her mother's side. The woman blubbered her thanks.

A crew of Imperial Police marched through the square, guns at the ready. The angry mob of extremists plowed into the open, setting off red-colored smoke bombs and shooting fire bullets through the windows of the governor's mansion. Bursts of ice blasted through the square, connecting with the drawn guns of the police and encasing the barrels. Chaos ensued as the swarm of extremists whipped Molotov cocktail bombs at the horde of police and released a wave of fire bullets onto them.

In the center of the army of extremists, he emerged.

Qiang.

Shiro's heart stopped for a moment. Qiang was alive. All the nights Shiro had spent crying over the possibility of the love of his life being dead were suddenly for naught. Here Qiang was, his muscles lean, his black hair hanging a bit longer than Shiro remembered, and scruff covered his square jaw. His thick brows were drawn. He was clearly present and determined. And he was alive.

Shiro's heart sped up again. It hammered in his chest and threatened to crack him into pieces. Qiang was leading the extremists into a dance with danger. He was making fatal moves with grave consequences.

"We've got to get these people out of here," Jae said through the earpiece.

"I've just cleared out the south quarter," Kamal announced. "Headed your way."

"I've calmed the people by the bridge," Yuki said. She had the advantage of her diamond mage powers to help control the emotions of the crowd near her. "The last of them are safely out of range."

Qiang marched closer, shouting orders and instructing his troops. With his crimson powers, he shook the ground and brought the oncoming police to their knees. Peng and Bao, the long-legged emerald mages who took part in their prison escape, used their powers to choke the first row of police officers. Mitty, the burly golden mage, tossed firebombs from his glowing palms over the cast-iron fence onto the lawn of the governor's mansion.

Shiro longed to call out to Qiang, but he feared

getting caught in the crossfire. Besides, he needed to get the people in the square to safety. Taking a deep breath, he summoned his powers. He wasn't sure what good it would do, but he was willing to try anything at this point. Clouds moved in and rain began to trickle down. The drops spotted Yuki's headscarf as she rushed toward Shiro.

"Everything's going to be okay," she said to the frightened people around Shiro, gesturing with her palms, which were aglow in bright white, for the stragglers to depart the area.

Shiro helped the young mother by guiding the little girl to follow her.

The rain came down faster, making it hard for the extremists to clearly see the barrage of Imperial Police charging in from out of nowhere.

Shiro couldn't help himself. He followed Qiang's movements as he fought off the police. Shiro made his move once the opportunity arose and darted toward Qiang. In his vigilance to stand his ground, Qiang raised his palms toward Shiro, ready to fight. But the second he realized it was Shiro coming toward him, his mouth hung open and he dropped his hands.

Shiro grabbed Qiang and hurriedly pushed him back and out of harm's way. They ducked behind a large statue of the sun god Surya.

Qiang placed his hands on the sides of Shiro's face. "How can this be?"

"You're alive."

Qiang let out a laugh. "That's what I was going to say. I thought you were shot."

"I *was* shot."

"But you live." Qiang pulled him closer and wrapped his arms around him.

Shiro squeezed him tightly and closed his eyes. Gunshots rang in his ears.

"Qiang." Shiro pulled back and searched his face. "What are you doing?"

"What do you mean?"

"This." Shiro gestured at the mansion. "These attacks."

"We can't let them get away with what they're doing, Shiro. Our families are still imprisoned. They have the grounds to deem mages illegal. We need to fight for our rights."

"But this way? It's dangerous. There were families out

here. Children. You're not considering the innocent lives you might be destroying."

Qiang searched his eyes, his expression grim. "Shiro, we're in a war. War has casualties."

"But if we can prevent innocent people from being killed—"

"Survival and freedom come at a price."

Shiro's brows dropped. "Is that why you gave up on me? Why it was so easy for you to accept that I was dead? Because lives are expendable during war?"

Qiang put his hands on Shiro's shoulders. "Shiro, no."

Shiro shrugged him off, his jaw tightening. A crackle in his earpiece interrupted his next sentence.

"Shiro! Yuki!" Jae sounded out of breath. "We've got to go. Kamal's been shot!"

Fourteen

It wasn't the mumbled voices in the temple that woke Loni; it was Kamal's grunts and moans. She covered her head with her pillow, begging the noise to stop. Every sound was like a giant needle being driven into her skull. Eventually, Kamal grew quiet, but the mumbling persisted.

Loni felt a wave of nausea as she forced herself out of bed. Her head pounded with every cruel beat of her heart. Curiosity drove her to find out what all the noise was about, but more than that, she needed water. An ocean's worth of water, judging by the sandpaper feel of her throat.

She reached the bottom of the stairs just as Darshana was closing the door behind someone.

"Who was that?" Even speaking made Loni's head throb.

Darshana placed her hands together in front of her, palms touching. "The doctor."

"What… What happened? Is it Amalia?"

"No. It's Kamal. He's been shot."

The shock of the news partially cleared Loni's mind, letting her push aside her own pain for a moment. "Is he all right?"

"Come see for yourself." Darshana headed for the living room.

Loni was relieved to see Kamal conscious on the couch. His pants had been cut over his thigh, exposing a thick bandage taped to his leg.

"Kamal." Loni hurried to the couch and kneeled beside him. "What happened?"

She glanced around. The only mage missing was Penny. Mr. Kitaro stood near Darshana—which seemed to be the norm as of late—with his hands stuffed in his pockets and a frown on his face. The others were gathered around, looking beat. Kamal, on the other hand, seemed rather pleased to be doted on, Loni thought to herself.

"Extremists," Jae answered. "Kamal got caught in the crossfire."

"They were using some kind of mage-made bullets," Shiro said, "made of stone and fire."

"Seared right through me." Kamal sucked in a breath through his teeth. "You should have seen the look on the doctor's face when he pulled it out."

"He's actually lucky it didn't rupture his femoral artery," Mr. Kitaro added.

Loni looked him up and down. "But you're okay?"

"Not exactly." Kamal hung his arm over the back of the couch. "No one's even offered me a snack yet. I mean, what's a guy got to do around here to get a bag of chips?"

Yuki let out a small laugh. "I'll get you some. Just stop whining like a baby."

Mayhara bit back a smile. "He's on pain killers."

Loni turned to Shiro. "What happened with the extremists?"

Shiro ran a hand through his hair. "They attacked

right outside the governor's mansion. We managed to get the civilians out of there, but Kamal got hit."

"I've been monitoring the media channels," Mayhara said. "There aren't a lot of details in the news. Not yet, anyway. But apparently the rebels were cleared out."

"Does that mean they were arrested or killed?" Loni asked.

Salina sat down in the chair across from the couch. "I'm sure the media has been persuaded to bury the real story. Probably because they don't want anything ruining their gala."

Loni furrowed her brow, which sent a small wave of dizziness through her head. "Wait. They're still going through with it?"

Mayhara shrugged. "Apparently."

Shiro let out a defeated sigh. "Which makes me wonder if there's an underlying reason for the event."

"Either way," Jay said as he rested on the arm of the couch, "if the other daggers are stashed somewhere in the mansion, they might be planning to move them because of today's attack."

"Well, I hate to tell you this." Kamal fiddled with the cut hem of his ruined pants. "This bullet wound might cause a slight setback as far as my dance moves are concerned."

Yuki, coming back into the room, tossed the bag of chips in his lap. "You can't even hobble to the kitchen for a snack. There's no way you're going to that gala."

"No." Mr. Kitaro let out a chuckle. "A limp like that would certainly act as a hindrance."

"Jae will have to go instead," Darshana said. "We need a sapphire mage to get in the door."

Jae and Mayhara exchanged a quick glance.

"Yeah." Jae cleared his throat. "All right."

Loni's temperature seemed to rise. Her head swam, threatening to throw her off-kilter. It was a good thing she was kneeling on the floor. If Jae was taking Kamal's place, that meant she and Jae would be posing as a couple at the gala. She ignored the heat that scorched her cheeks.

"That's not the only alteration to the plan."

Everyone turned to look as Penny entered the room, Karina in tow.

Darshana narrowed her eyes. "What did you see?"

"A possibility," Penny said as she and Karina sat on the floor around the coffee table. "It's going to be tricky getting the daggers *and* leaving with them."

"You have a plan?" Mayhara asked, joining them on the floor.

"Karina does." Penny nodded at her.

"Penny kept envisioning different scenarios where the Pishacha and the dark mages catch you retrieving the daggers. The visions were different each time, but we're certain the Pishacha and dark mages will be at the gala."

"I don't like the feel of this," Yuki remarked.

"Neither do I," Karina said. "Which is why I came up with something that I hope will help. At least temporarily."

"Go on." Mr. Kitaro stepped closer.

Karina looked around at everyone. "I can do a boundary spell to trap them."

"What's a boundary spell?" Kamal asked.

"It's a spell that can seal someone—or in this case, a group of people—in a space for a certain amount of time. The mansion itself is too big to do the spell on without a powerful talisman or a celestial event."

"What about the comet?" Yuki asked.

"It's not close enough yet," Penny explained.

"But if the Pishacha and company can be led into one place—say, the room where the daggers are hidden—I can trap them there so you can escape without them being able to follow you."

"But what about their black-smoke disappearing trick?" Salina asked.

"They wouldn't be able to leave the boundaries of the room in any form, so if they did disappear, they'd only be able to reappear within the room."

"So cool," Kamal said.

"But there's a catch," Karina added.

"Figures," Shiro muttered.

"The spell I'm using pulls its magic from a special anointed candle. The boundary spell will only last as long as the candle burns."

Jae rubbed at his jaw. "How long is that?"

"It depends on how strong I need the spell to be. And I'm guessing, with the force of the entities in that room, it'll need to be a pretty strong spell."

Loni shifted, pulling her legs out from under her and gathering her knees closer to her body. "So we pretty much have to get out of there as fast as possible, just in case."

Karina nodded. "Pretty much."

"How are we going to make sure the Pishacha find

Jae and Loni?" Shiro asked. "That is, without drawing the attention of the governor and the Imperial Police and all?"

"Maybe I can help with that," Yuki said. She straightened her shoulders. "Avi is sure to be there. I'll make sure he sees me and lead him to the room. I'm sure the others will follow."

"We don't know for sure they'd follow." Salina rubbed her hands together. "But it could work. We'd have to time it just right, though."

"I'll talk them all through it with the earpieces Jae made," Penny said. "That way I can keep you apprised of how fast Karina's candle is burning."

They were all silent for a while, deep in thought. Loni felt a hard knot in her chest, and her fingers trembled slightly. This was a huge mission, and she was one of the key players. A mild sweat began to form on her brow. As her stomach began to churn, she tried to push away the craving for more Moxy to ease her nerves. But her addiction was putting up a fight.

At long last, Darshana spoke. "It's risky, yes, but I think it could work. The others can stand by outside of the mansion gate in case something goes awry."

"We have two days," Penny said. "If anyone thinks of anything we missed, you better bring it up before the plan goes into action."

As the rest of them agreed, Loni bit her lip. Her skin began to itch, and her heart felt heavy. She wasn't sure she could hold herself together enough to pull this off. She knew she had to, but it was going to be a challenge. And she couldn't shake the feeling that desperate times were calling for desperate measures.

Fifteen

Kashmeru's thumb traced small, delicate circles in Lakshmi's palm. She watched the strokes as her skin began to tingle and the tiny hairs sprung to life along her arms. When she looked up at him, his eyes were soft yet intense. And the small upturn of the corner of his mouth made her blush.

"When I'm with you," he said, "everything else fades away."

She smiled and averted her eyes, overwhelmed by the

feeling of joy inside of her.

"See how good it is when we are together?" he asked, moving closer.

"Yes," she replied, following his lead and closing the distance between them.

She could feel his breath on her lips, but at the last second, he pulled away. She blinked at him in surprise.

His smile disappeared. "Perhaps next time, you won't fail."

"What?"

Naree sat upright, stirred back to the present. Kashmeru had finally spoken to her after a silence that seemed like forever. But his message was clear. He was disappointed in her failure to secure all the daggers, but he was giving her another chance.

"Kashmeru," she called from the sofa where she had fallen asleep earlier. "I'm sorry."

I know, my love.

Her heart practically burst with gratitude that he had answered her.

I believe you have learned your lesson and will do as I wish.

"Of course. Anything for you."

We will be together soon. You just need to get the daggers so we can begin the ritual. The reward will be worth it, I promise you.

Tears spilled over her lashes, but her smile reflected her delight. She wanted to be with him again. To feel his thumb trace circles in her palm. To be near him again and not have him pull away from their kiss.

The door to the lounge opened, and Bhutano marched in.

"Your highness." He gave her a slight bow.

This time, she was not afraid of what he would say. Kashmeru was with her again, and this was her chance to prove to him that she would succeed. To prove her love to him.

She stood, holding her chin high. "Yes?"

"There's been an attack on the governor's mansion. Extremists."

She hadn't been prepared for this news. She furrowed her brow, trying to wrap her head around it. "Did they get inside?"

"No."

"Was anyone hurt? Avi?"

"Avi is unharmed. But we lost a couple Imperial

Police in the chaos. The area is secured now, and measures are being taken to ensure the mansion can't be infiltrated."

She had to be certain the daggers hidden in the mansion weren't taken. If they were, she'd lose any footing they had in this battle.

"We need to stop them from further endangering our plan," she said.

"I agree. I've sent a team of Pishacha on a manhunt. We will find them and eradicate the situation. We're also discussing the destruction of the prison camps. With the mage families trapped behind the walls."

She flinched. "How will you carry that out?"

"We're devising a plan. It might take a bit of time to coordinate in a way so as not to turn the public against the government. We want to pin the blame on the extremists."

"Do you think the public will believe the extremists would destroy their own people?"

"We hope to make it appear as if the deaths of the mage families are collateral damage. That the extremists meant to attack the camp guards but destroyed everything and everyone in their path instead."

She inhaled deeply, considering the plan. "It could work. But I'm also concerned about the daggers."

"I'll discuss moving them to a more secure location with the governor. I'm certain we can come up with a solution."

She nodded, her mind whirring.

"As for the remaining daggers," he said, studying her face. "I have an idea in which you play a vital role."

Sixteen

Crickets chirped, filling the night air with their song. Jae watched Mayhara's face as she gazed at the comet. Moonlight shimmered on her features, like tiny sparkles he wanted to chase with his lips. She'd been quiet all day, and he wondered if she might have regretted their kiss.

They'd spent the day training, honing their skills for the possible showdown at the gala the next day. Though she'd smiled at him whenever he looked her way, he couldn't help but think the smile didn't quite reach her eyes. Of course, he could just be paranoid. After all, this plan of theirs was risky. Mayhara's distance could simply be the way she dealt with worry.

"What are you thinking about?" Jae kept his voice low and soft.

Mayhara tucked a strand of hair behind her ear. "When I was little, my father and I would sit outside when it got dark and watch for shooting stars. Then, as I began to come into my powers, I saw one, and I wished that I would become the best crimson mage there ever was."

He smiled at her. "And now you are."

She nodded. "Now I am. And I didn't expect to feel so overwhelmed."

Taking her hand, Jae stroked her skin with his thumb. "Have you already forgotten what we said? We're in this together. You're not fighting this fight alone."

She smiled back at him and squeezed his hand.

The buzz of Jae's Linq interrupted them. Jae's brows pulled together when he saw Loni's number appear on the screen. He spared Mayhara a glance before he answered.

"Yeah?"

"Jae, I need help." Loni breathed hard into the Linq.

"Where are you?"

"Downtown New Jaipur."

"What? I didn't even know you left the temple."

"Jae. Please. I think I'm being followed."

"Okay. Ping me your location. I'll come get you." He hung up, a stiffness in his neck and jaw.

"Who was that?" Mayhara asked.

He let out a hard sigh. "It was Loni. She's in New Jaipur."

"What? Why?"

He was reluctant to answer. A slow anger bubbled up inside of him. If his suspicions were correct, Loni had fallen into her old habits again. Or perhaps she'd never given them up at all.

He shook his head. "I need to go get her."

"I'll come with you."

"It'll be faster on my bike. She thinks someone might be following her. If so, I can evade them easier on my bike."

Mayhara blinked and crossed her hands over her chest. "Oh. Okay. Be careful."

"I will. "

He leaned closer to her, hesitantly. When she didn't pull away, he kissed her gently on the lips. It was just a peck, but it was somehow reassuring. He nodded his goodbye and headed for the carport.

Dashing to his bike, he clenched his teeth. It was typical of Loni to get into trouble. As long as he'd known her, she had never been able to avoid it. And this wasn't the first time he'd had to pull her out of it.

He was still searing with anger by the time he found her almost an hour later. She stood near an old, out-of-service vending machine at an abandoned gas station, keeping to the shadows with a sweatshirt hood pulled low over her face. She looked over her shoulder as she shuffled to his bike.

She stumbled when she reached him. Jae stuck out his arm and caught her before she could fall.

As she straightened out, he pulled off his helmet and studied her. "Are you okay?"

She shivered. "I don't know."

"Look at me."

When she didn't listen to him, he grabbed her by her shoulders. She gasped and gaped at him. Her eyes were wide and bloodshot. She pressed her lips together and began tipping to the side, her lids drooping closed.

He knew it. She was high.

"Loni!" he shouted through his teeth. "How could you do this?"

There was a *crash* nearby, like a metal trash can had been knocked over. They both turned their heads, scanning the dark for movement. Though he was still fuming, he knew they shouldn't stick around.

"Come on." He handed her the spare helmet. "Let's go."

As soon as she was securely on the bike, her hands holding his side, he revved his engine and took off. The streets downtown were in bad shape, so he swerved around potholes and braced himself as they maneuvered over gravel-covered cement.

He heard another engine approaching. A glance in his side mirror led him to let out a curse and speed up. The headlights of the car behind him were getting closer.

"Hold on." He wasn't sure if Loni had heard him, but her grip stayed true.

Up ahead, the lampposts on either side of the street began to bend into the road.

Dark mages!

Jae flew toward the next intersection. He sped up and veered right, hopping up on the sidewalk. Cutting the corner, he heard the squealing tires of the pursuing car. They weren't happy with his stunt, and their own magic got in the way of their chase.

Jae hunkered down as his speed increased, and Loni's hold on him became tighter.

The car wasn't far behind. He had to lose them. There was no returning to the temple with dark mages on his tail.

He skidded sideways and zoomed into an alleyway, cutting between buildings. The car screeched to a stop, but the crates, barrels, and dumpsters in the alley began moving into the center of Jae's path. He had to zigzag to dodge them, barely scraping by. Loni let out a whimper. All this movement had to be brutal on her, especially in her state of mind. He was just glad she hadn't let go.

After they broke free from the alley, Jae skidded into another turn and raced to the next intersection. He was sure the dark mages following him would be clever enough to go around the block to catch up with them, so there was no slowing down now.

When he turned the next corner, he spotted a construction site ahead of them. He used his sapphire powers to quiet the motor.

"Loni, I'm going to need your help."

She stiffened. "Okay."

"See that work site up the street?" He felt her shift behind him.

"Yeah."

"Big mountain of dirt?"

He felt her let go with one hand. "Got it."

He hoped she understood what we wanted her to do, because a glance in his side mirror told him their pursuers were not far behind them. As they neared the construction site, an emerald glow appeared behind him. Dirt kicked up and floated into the air. At the same time, the scaffolding surrounding the building began to shake, metal poles detaching from the structure and flying toward the road. Jae knew this move had been caused by the dark mages.

"Loni!"

"I'm trying!"

The wind picked up. The particles from the mountain of dirt began to swirl as they rose, forming what looked like a tornado. Loni grunted, and the tornado moved toward the road, behind the bike and in front of the car. Small bits of debris struck Jae's helmet, but they'd cleared the whirlwind. Jae watch in his side mirror as the car flipped on its side from the swirling storm of dirt and debris.

Not wanting to take any chances, he shifted into top gear and raced out of the city before anyone else could catch them.

Seventeen

Jae barged into the temple, gritting his teeth. He told himself to calm down. Loni was a wreck, and chances were she wouldn't even remember half of what had happened tonight. He went into the kitchen to get some water. Loni followed. As he sipped his water, she simply stood there, not saying a word. She rubbed at the skin under her eyes, which were still bloodshot.

"What happened, Loni?" He didn't yell. He didn't want to wake the whole house.

She crossed her arms. "I don't know."

"How could you risk this? Especially after what happened to Kamal. We can't afford to lose any more manpower. We can't afford to lose an elite."

"You never got it, did you?" She raised her arms and dropped them at her sides. "The pressure is crippling."

"Of course I get it. But you don't see the rest of us giving in to our demons to deal with the pressure."

"Well, maybe I'm not cut from the same cloth as the rest of you. Maybe I'm not as put-together as everyone else."

His hands were clenched into fists, but he kept them at his sides. "How did you even pay for it?"

She averted her gaze.

"Loni."

"I traded for it." Her voice was so quiet, he almost hadn't heard it.

"Traded what?" When she didn't answer, Jae scrubbed a hand down his face. He'd lived this before. She'd stolen from strangers—and from friends, no less— to pay for drugs. She'd always felt horrible afterward, but it had definitely made Jae lose his trust in her. "Did you take something from one of us?"

"No."

He narrowed his eyes at her.

"Not from one of you." She sighed. "I took one of the small golden trinkets from the dining room."

"So you thought: house full of fancy things, easy way to get something worth trading for drugs?"

"You don't understand. I have no control over it. I can't stop it. Believe me, I'm trying. But my sister... I can't get her out of my head. It's like there's something evil inside me and it's clawing at my old wounds and ripping them open again."

"That's no excuse, Loni. We're in a war."

"Exactly. There's so much pressure."

They both turned as Mayhara walked into the kitchen. Her eyes darted between them. "What's going on?"

Loni wiped her tears from her face and looked away from her.

Jae rubbed the back of his neck. "It's… Don't worry about it."

Mayhara's brow wrinkled. "I don't understand. Loni, what were you doing in New Jaipur? Does this have anything to do with why you left the temple a few nights ago?"

Jae set his jaw. "You've done this more than once since you've been here? Loni, this is an addiction. Can't you see?"

"Addiction?" Mayhara studied Loni, who wouldn't look at her. "Are you…? Is this about drugs?"

Loni rolled her eyes. "Listen, Miss Perfect. You know nothing about me."

Mayhara scoffed. "Is that why you were out there? To get a fix? Drugs are so important to you that you would put us all in danger?"

"It's my own business," Loni said through gritted teeth.

"No." Mayhara pressed on her temples. "It could affect us all. You not realizing that is selfish. And selfishness is not a luxury any of us can afford."

Jae stepped between them. "Okay, that's enough."

Mayhara narrowed her eyes. "What? Jae, you're defending her?"

He let out a sigh. "You don't know the whole story."

"I don't feel I have to. This could endanger our whole—"

"Mayhara, drop it. Please."

His voice was stern, and Mayhara flinched. Loni raked her hair away from her face.

Mayhara looked between them and lifted her chin. "Fine."

She turned and marched out of the kitchen.

"Mayhara," Jae called, but she didn't look back. He planted his hands on his waist and glared at Loni.

"Don't give me that look," Loni said. "I don't need your judgement, and I don't need you to defend me."

She knocked a bamboo bowl off the counter before she stomped away.

Kamal suddenly appeared, hobbling in on crutches. He grabbed a cookie from the cookie jar and then leaned back against the counter. "Chicks. Am I right?"

"Shut up, Kamal."

Jae hurried out of the room. He needed to catch up with Mayhara. Darting up the stairs, he hoped she'd give him a chance to explain. He sucked in a breath as he tapped lightly on her door, praying to the gods she wouldn't ignore him.

His shoulders dropped in relief when she opened the door. But the look she gave him made his stomach churn.

"Mayhara, I'm sorry. Can we talk?"

She pressed her lips together, simply looking at him for a moment. Fear rose in his veins that she'd turn him away. But then, by some miracle, she nodded.

"Yeah, sure." She opened the door wider and turned away, walking toward her window.

He walked halfway into the room. The last time he'd been in here, they'd shared a kiss. "I should explain why I stopped you from berating Loni."

"Berating?" She scoffed. "Jae, she could have ended this all for us. You said she thought she was being followed, and the only thing I can think of is that the Pishacha or dark mages found her."

He stuffed his hands in his pockets. "Yeah. She was being followed by dark mages. But we lost them."

"But the fact that she went out there in the first place—for drugs, no less—was a bad move."

"I know. Believe me, I told her that."

"So it's just that you didn't think *I* should tell her that? You think we should have an elite who's hooked on drugs?"

He took a step toward her, but she took a step back. He pushed a hand through his hair and dropped his gaze. "I just... I thought it would just make it worse if we ganged up on her. I was already giving her the shame speech."

"So, because you have some history with her, you thought it should be you."

He flinched at her words. He'd never mentioned having a history with Loni to Mayhara. "Did she say something to you?"

Mayhara averted her gaze and shook her head. "No. But it's true, right? You have a history?"

He nodded slowly.

She crossed her arms. "Maybe you should tell me about it."

"The day of the Eradication, we escaped together."

She took a deep breath and let it out. "Okay."

"We stayed hidden until the Imperial Police left, and then we ran away. But something else happened that day. Loni's sister, Kanya, was killed. Right in front of her eyes. And there was nothing either of us could do to stop it. And she carried that with her when we escaped. We sheltered in a few obscure places as we made our way to her family, and we got close. We grew to depend on each other and became comfortable with each other's company. But she would cry at night and have nightmares about Kanya being killed, and then one day, she began disappearing for hours at a time in the middle of the night."

"She was going out to get drugs."

He nodded. "When I found out, we fought. I told her this wasn't the way to deal with her grief. And at first it worked. I thought she was clean when we got to her parents' place. But she had to tell them about Kanya, and she had to tell them they needed to find a place to hide from the government. They'd started arresting the families of mages and placing them in prison camps."

Mayhara rubbed at her arms, slightly hunched over as she thought about her own parents, still trapped behind the walls of their prison camp.

"We helped them pack up," Jae continued. "And I was supposed to bring her to join them in a hidden cottage in the mountains before I headed back to Korea. But having to see the looks on their faces when they learned they'd lost a daughter... For Loni to have to explain to them that she'd watched her sister die... Well, it wasn't long before she turned to something that would numb the pain again. I tried to stick by her and break her of the habit, but she's an addict. She went behind my back. Finally, I couldn't deal with it anymore, and I told her she had to choose. She didn't choose me. And after that, I never saw her again. That is, until she showed up with the other elites at the observatory."

Mayhara watched him a bit longer. After a while, she uncrossed her arms. "It's a sad story," she said softly. "I'm sorry for her loss."

"I didn't know she was still doing it."

Mayhara pursed her lips. "Maybe I should go with you to the gala."

"No, that's too dangerous. If they recognize you, you'll be arrested. Or worse."

Her brows sunk down, heat rising in her throat. "Is that the real reason? Or is it you'd rather go with Loni?"

He tried to close the distance between them. "Mayhara—"

She backed away. "You know, I knew you two had a past. But I had to find out from Kamal. *Kamal*, Jae. Do you have any idea what that felt like?"

"I didn't think it was important. That was in the past."

"Was it?" She shook her head. "It looked like you were more than happy to defend her just now."

He took another step toward her.

She held up her hands. "No. I need some space. This is…" She scoffed. "This is not right. We should be concentrating on getting the daggers. Not on a silly fling."

"Mayhara."

"I said *no*. This"—she gestured between them—"is not why we're here. Not why I'm here. We need to beat Kashmeru. We need to ensure the safety of our families. Of the world. So that's the only thing I'm going to be putting my efforts into."

She marched to her door and held it, waiting for him to leave. She wouldn't look at him as he walked past her, and he could feel his heart crack into an infinite number of pieces as she closed the door behind him.

Eighteen

Mayhara refused to cry any more. It had been an hour, and she was out of tissues. She didn't want to wonder anymore if Jae still had feelings for Loni. She didn't want to concentrate on the fact that Loni was the one who'd ended it. She didn't choose Jae. It had probably broken his heart. It didn't matter. There were more important things at hand. Yet she couldn't ignore the tightness in her chest. There was no denying she had feelings for him, and their relationship fizzling out before it even had a chance to begin made her heart sink. But she had to find the will to tuck away those feelings, just for now, just for the moment.

A knock on her door made her jump. Though she didn't want to fight with Jae anymore, she couldn't stop herself from answering. Deep down, she wanted to see him.

She blinked in surprise when she opened the door to find Salina.

"Oh," Mayhara said. "Hi. It's the middle of the night."

"I know." Salina grimaced. "Sorry. But I wanted to see if you were okay."

Mayhara grimaced. "Did you hear us fighting? I'm so embarrassed."

"Don't be embarrassed. Tensions are high around here."

Mayhara let out the smallest of laughs. "You could say that."

"Did you break up?"

Mayhara bit her lip. "Come in."

Salina stepped into her room and sat on the corner of

the bed. "I thought you might want to talk."

Mayhara wrapped her arms around herself. "What's there to talk about, really? We weren't even really together, were we? It was just one kiss. Well, two. But the second one was just—you know what? It's not important."

"That doesn't mean it doesn't hurt," Salina said. "I see the way he looks at you."

"It doesn't matter." Mayhara rubbed at her eyes. "I can't think about that right now. I'm the root mage; I need to stay grounded. What the hell am I doing, putting matters of the heart in front of the fate of the world?"

They were quiet for a moment, and then Salina sighed.

"We used to be friends, you know? Loni and I."

Mayhara sat next to her on the bed. "Used to be? What happened?"

Salina opened her mouth to speak, but instead of words, a sob escaped her lips. She covered her face with her hands as tears began to fall.

Mayhara leaned closer to her. "Salina, what happened?"

Salina took her hand and shook her head. "I'm sorry.

I'm sorry. This wasn't supposed to be about me."

"No, it's okay. Don't worry."

"It's just… It's Huojin."

"Salina, it's okay. It hasn't been that long. We're all still torn up about it, but you were her best friend. It makes sense that you—out of everyone—must still be the most devastated over her death."

"I thought I was holding myself together so well."

"But you don't have to. You're allowed to grieve." Mayhara pulled her in for a hug.

For a moment, Mayhara forgot about her fight with Jae. She let Salina cry on her shoulder, shedding tears herself for their fallen friend.

When she released her, Salina gave her a small smile.

"Did you still want to tell me about you and Loni?" Mayhara asked.

Salina nodded, sniffling back the last of her tears. "We actually became friends through Huojin."

"Really?"

"Huojin and Loni's sister, Kanya, were a couple. But Kanya was very temperamental, and Huojin was very stubborn, so it didn't last. They had a bad breakup. Two strong personalities like that… It got hostile."

"I don't think I ever noticed."

Salina swiped at her cheeks. "They mostly fought in the golden mage dorms. They didn't want Darshana to find out. Anyway, the breakup ended up pitting Loni and me against each other."

"How awful."

"The comments and criticisms between the four of us got out of control and became aggressive, and one day Loni got in Huojin's face, and I wanted her to back off. My temper got the best of me and I… I accidentally burned her arm."

Mayhara's eyes widened. "You *burned* Loni?"

"I hadn't meant to. I apologized, but she didn't want to hear it."

"After all this time, she may have put it behind her."

"I don't know." Salina shrugged. "She doesn't exactly have friendly conversations with me now. I don't think we're in a good place yet."

Mayhara shook her head. "Loni's just not in a good place, period."

Salina grimaced. "I heard."

"You did? From whom?"

"Kamal."

Mayhara raised a brow. "Of course."

"I guess Jae wasn't enough comfort for her to deal with her grief. So she turned to drugs."

Mayhara let out a sigh. "I can understand she's fighting an addiction, and I guess I should have some sympathy regarding that. I just hope she doesn't let that get in the way of our mission." Mayhara shook her head. "Otherwise, we're never going to win the battle, let alone the war.

Nineteen

Fireworks filled the night sky. They would be set off all night, as was tradition at the governor's mansion on gala night during the Navratri festival. But this time, the celebration was bigger, as a symbol of welcoming the Akutake comet.

The governor and his staff had certainly pulled strings to get the broken windows replaced and the damage to the property covered up in time for the party.

Everywhere Loni looked, people were dressed in

extravagant ballgowns, dashing tuxedos, and, most importantly, gorgeous and elaborate masks to hide their faces. Some attendees even wore top hats or fascinators to complete their look. She was surrounded by glitter, feathers, and flowing champagne.

"Are you all right?" Jae asked her.

Her arm was hooked through his as they entered the mansion. She fought to ignore the churn in her stomach. "Yeah. Sure."

"You're supposed to be enjoying yourselves," Yuki said from behind them. "Maybe smile or something?"

Loni's earpiece crackled. "Let us know your progress," Penny said. "Karina's got everything prepared for the spell here. Yuki, remember: You've got to place the talisman in the room we want to trap them in."

"Yep," Yuki answered softly. "Got it."

They'd made it to the front porch without incident, but they were approaching the door, where every guest was being checked off a list.

"Looks like you're up," Loni said to Jae, faking a smile.

"Don't worry. I'll help," Yuki said.

Loni glanced over her shoulder to see that Yuki was

smiling. And something told her it wasn't fake.

"Name, please." The woman at the door wore a black-and-yellow ballgown and held a clipboard. Her mask was one that had to be held up with a stick, but she simply kept it in her hand with the clipboard, probably tired of lifting it between talking to every guest.

Jae put his hands behind his back. Loni moved closer to Jae to block the view as he called upon his sapphire powers.

"You don't need our names," Jae whispered to the woman. "The three of us are welcome to join the party."

Yuki leaned forward. "And you're very happy to see us."

Loni resisted the urge to roll her eyes.

The woman blinked at Jae and then grinned. "Welcome to the party! I'm so glad you could join us."

Jae's smile was genuine this time. He bowed graciously to the woman and then proceeded inside with Loni and Yuki in tow.

"Why do I feel like I'm part of a vampire gang?" Loni asked.

"Good thing she invited us in, right?" Jae joked.

The foyer was lit by an elegant chandelier. Loni was

willing to bet it was normally the center of attraction when entering the mansion, but tonight it had to compete with the barrage of paper lanterns, dragon steamers, and bamboo-paper hanging fans that decorated everywhere one looked. Ikebana flower arrangements were displayed on marble pedestals.

Travelling farther into the house, Loni realized most of the décor was based on New Jaipur's flag colors: red, yellow, white, green, and blue. Beads with these colors were strung around the staircase handrails, laid out on tablecloths, and hung from the ceiling. The decorating team had also lain out LED strips along the baseboards to create a mystical ambiance.

"Mayhara? Shiro?" Penny's voice came over their earpieces. "You're in position?"

"All clear here," Shiro answered. He and Mayhara were waiting by the cars, ready to take off as soon as the daggers were acquired.

"Your attention, please."

The voice came from the ballroom. Loni, Jae, and Yuki worked their way into the grand room to find a woman standing near the large, glass, double patio doors in a deep red ballgown with a plume of feathers in her hair.

"That's Shei," Jae whispered to Loni and Yuki. "Mayhara's old boss at the census company. She's involved with the Pishacha. Her daughter is a dark mage."

"I have the honor of welcoming you all to this year's Navratri Festival Gala," Shei said. "Governor Laghari and his family and staff have been organizing this gala for six months now, and despite attempts to thwart our efforts, the gala has commenced with success."

The crowd applauded. As Shei introduced the governor to address the partygoers, Loni studied the people surrounding him. Shei said something to the young woman beside her. She was willing to bet the girl in the silver dress was her daughter, Ru. She recognized the young man whispering in Ru's ear as Harish Patel, the son of the wealthiest man in New Jaipur. He had a narrow face and a prominent nose, and there was almost a wildness in his eyes as he glanced around the room. Loni made a note to keep an eye on him. There was something about him that gave Loni the feeling he was also a dark mage. The way these groups were intertwined, it wouldn't surprise her. Slightly behind the governor stood his wife and his son, Avi. Loni recognized him from the news. He had a boyish face, with thick lips and a narrow chin, but his body was pure lean muscle. His mane of dark brown hair spiked out from his head in one direction She could see why Yuki had been interested in him.

Once Loni and Jae found the room the daggers were in, Yuki would have to lead these three—and any Pishacha who might be around—into the room so that Karina's spell could trap them. Loni wondered if the other four dark mages were at the party.

"As soon as you see the fireplace, let me know," Penny said into their ears. "I'll describe what I saw in my vision and lead you to the room."

The crowd applauded again as the governor ended his speech. "Thank you, everyone. Please, enjoy the party."

Music began to play. Yuki moved closer to Loni and Jae. "Okay, you two try to look inconspicuous while I search for that fireplace."

"Good luck," Loni told her.

Jae lifted his chin, staring into space for a moment.

"Jae?"

He shifted his attention back to her. "Come on. Let's dance."

She was surprised when he took her hand and led her

to the dancefloor. He seemed to be bringing her to a specific spot. She glanced around and realized they weren't far from where Governor Laghari, Director Shei, and the chief of police were sipping champagne and conversing.

Jae swung around to face Loni and assumed a dancing stance, his hands on her waist. It was a familiar feeling, having his hands on her. She'd almost forgotten how right it felt. Though she wished he would, he wasn't looking into her eyes. She knew he was eavesdropping on the conversation being held with the governor.

"The chief of police is asking Shei if she's secured a place to move the daggers." Jae spoke in a low voice so only Loni—and the other mages listening in—could hear.

As they turned in their dance, Loni glanced over to the chief of police. The governor's brows were drawn as he spoke.

"Governor Laghari is reluctant to move them until the festivities are over," Jae said. "Too many eyes."

"Okay," Loni said. "But at least we know they're still here."

Jae stiffened. "Oh my God."

"What?" Loni asked.

Her earpiece clicked. "What's wrong, Jae?"

Jae swallowed hard. "The governor just called the chief of police 'Bhutano.'"

Loni's jaw almost dropped. "Bhutano? As in Kashmeru's spirit messenger?"

"Yeah." Jae spared the man a glance. He stood tall, his shoulders broad, his hair extremely short, and he kept his lips in a straight line. "We thought he'd been possessing a man named Bruno, whom Naree was seeing before she fell under Kashmeru's spell—or because of his spell, I can't be sure. But we beat Bruno in a fight, and he disappeared like the Pishacha do, and Bhutano was apparently still around. Looks like we were wrong about his identity."

"I guess it makes sense," Loni said, "with the way the police and the government are mixed up in this."

"Bhutano says he's sent out some of his dark mages to get rid of the extremist. The ones who were not expected to be at the gala."

"So that means they're not here. Hopefully, they're not near enough to interfere with our plan."

Jae bit the inside of his cheek.

"What now?" Loni asked.

"They're talking about taking care of the prison camps, but I don't know what they mean. Something they've been planning to do. I'm afraid they want to destroy them—and everyone inside of them."

Loni froze in place, nearly stumbling mid-dance. "They can't do that."

"What's stopping them?" Jae urged her to continue dancing.

Loni dropped her gaze. Destroying the prison camps would mean the deaths of millions of mage families. "What do you think will happen to the government if we beat Kashmeru?"

Jae took a deep breath and let it out. "If we can get the empress where she belongs—on the throne and in charge—order should be restored. Naree will deem mages legal again, the prison camps will fall, families will be released, and if there's any justice in the world, those who were involved with the Pishacha will be removed from their positions."

Loni looked around at all the masked women in the room. "Do you think Naree is here?"

"I don't know. If she is, it would be hard to recognize

her."

Loni's hands trembled, and she felt a dull ache in her head. Her addiction was calling to her. It was her body's response to dealing with the stress. But she had to push the craving away. She had to concentrate on the task at hand. Glancing at Jae, she decided to change the subject to keep her mind off the threat of nausea.

She adjusted her mask. "It's funny. All that time we spent together and you never mentioned that your sister was the Lotus."

"I had to keep it a secret."

"Even from me?"

Jae averted his gaze. "You weren't exactly trustworthy, sneaking off in the middle of the night, getting yourself into trouble."

Her shoulders hunched and her cheeks burned. "I'm sorry, you know?"

"Loni." Jae shook his head, letting out a humorless laugh. "Now's not the time."

"I know. I just… I just need you to know that. I was stupid. When you told me to choose between my vices and you? Choosing my vices… That was the stupidest decision I ever made in my life."

Jae gazed at her for a moment. She wished she could see his whole face. She wished she could tell what he was thinking. After a moment, he broke eye contact and looked over her shoulder.

"Are you… feeling better?"

She sighed. "I don't even know what that means anymore. The word 'normal' is lost on me."

"Guys." It was Yuki's voice on the earpiece. "I found the fireplace."

Jae stopped dancing and slowly led Loni out of the ballroom.

"You sure it's the right one?" Penny asked.

"Two tall cast-iron candle holders stood on either side," Yuki said. "A painting of a girl smelling a lotus."

"Yep, that's it," Penny said.

"We're on our way, Yuki." Jae took his time getting through the crowd. They didn't want to draw too much attention by rushing. They feigned smiles and acted polite as they wormed through silk and beads and feathers to get to where Yuki was.

"Okay," Jae said. "Let's find the room and make sure the daggers are in there before we lure the dark mages in."

"It's a hall to the right," Penny told them. "Second

door on the left."

As they made their way toward the door, they discovered two security guards standing sentry in the hall, along with a handful of gossiping partygoers.

"My turn," Loni said. "Try not to breathe too deeply for a sec."

She felt the power in her palms as she diminished the air in the hall. The people who were congregating there began to clear their throats. The men pulled at their collars, and the women patted at their throats. One by one, they departed the hall.

The guards, though visibly uncomfortable, stood their ground.

Jae approached them, his palms glowing blue. "Looks like you two need to go out and get some air."

Loni released her hold on the air pressure as the guards left their stations.

"What's the code, Penny?" Loni asked.

After getting the door open, she, Jae, and Yuki entered the room.

Jae gestured at a door at the far end of the room. "That must be it."

Penny gave them the code for this door as well. Loni's

heart pounded as the door clicked open and they slipped inside. It was a walk-in closet with shelves. On one of the shelves were three black-and-red boxes. Jae opened one of them to confirm.

"We've found them," he said.

Yuki walked up to the shelves and took a small charm out of her clutch purse. It was a round, wooden charm with the image of a flame engraved into it. Karina had charged the figure with a magical force to connect it to the candle she was about to burn.

"The talisman's in place," Yuki said.

"Karina has started the spell," Penny told them.

"I'll go get Avi's attention." Yuki tilted her head and left the room.

"Let's take these, then." Jae removed the first dagger from the box and slipped it into the inside pocket of his tuxedo jacket.

Loni took the next dagger and placed it in a secret pocket in the skirt of her dress as Jae secured the final dagger.

"I can't believe we've got them all," Loni whispered.

"Let's not get too confident yet." He adjusted his lapels. "We've got to get out of here first."

"Okay, he sees me," Yuki said. "Headed your way. The other two are with him."

Black smoke burst in the room, and Jae and Loni flinched when two Pishacha appeared.

"I guess word travels fast," Loni said.

As the Pishacha approached, Loni mustered all her strength and threw out a wave of her power. The two Pishacha froze, grabbing their chests. They both disappeared, black smoke swirling.

"What was that?" Jae asked.

"I sucked the air out of their hearts. I don't like doing that; it's draining."

Yuki ran into the room, spinning around to face the door just as Avi, Ru, and Harish stomped in behind her. Avi squared his jaw and raised his palms.

"Watch out!" Yuki shouted, stepping in front of Jae and Loni and throwing her diamond shield between them and the dark mages. "Avi's a bone crusher. Stay behind the shield."

"Penny," Jae said. "How's it looking?"

"Karina's almost done. She needs another minute."

Loni held her palms up. Avi's eyes widened. He threw his hands around his neck and gasped. As he dropped to his knees, the two Pishacha who had disappeared reappeared at Avi's side. Ru held her palm up, and framed pictures that hung on the wall tore away and zipped through the air. One hit Yuki on the side of the head. Her diamond shield dropped.

The Pishacha advanced.

Jae threw out a blast of sound. Everyone in the room covered their ears, including Loni and Yuki. He hadn't had time to warn them. Harish held his palms up, and all the lights in the room burst. Electricity flashed in the air.

"Penny!" Jae yelled.

"Okay, go," Penny said. "But the candle is burning faster than we anticipated. You need to book it."

Loni raised her palms again and then closed her hands into tight fists. The three dark mages and the two Pishacha gasped as they clutched at their hearts, backing away.

"Go!" she screamed, grabbing Yuki's hand and pulling her out of the room.

Jae was close behind. As they made it into the hallway, they looked over their shoulders just long enough to see the Pishacha disappearing and reappearing in the room, filling it with smoke as they tried to escape.

The three dark mages were in shock, because they couldn't get past the doorway.

"Come on," Jae said. "Don't run. It'll look suspicious."

He raised his palm once more and aimed it at the doorway. The yells and hollers from within the room were suddenly silenced.

"The candle is almost out," Penny said.

"We're headed out the front door as we speak," Jae said.

Twenty

Penny let out a long breath and took the earpiece out of her ear. "They made it. They're on their way."

Karina nodded, staring at the wick of the candle that was no longer aflame. "That was close."

Penny glanced at the others, not yet able to relax. Inside of her, the anxiety of the situation still bubbled. She'd have to find a chance to meditate to clear the unwelcome feeling from her body.

"They got the daggers?" Darshana asked.

"Yeah, they got them," Penny answered.

"Brilliant," Mr. Kitaro said, straightening his blazer.

"I can't believe the chief of police is Bhutano," Salina said, sitting on the couch with her hands pressed between her knees. "No wonder the police are against us."

"All this excitement has made me hungry," Kamal said. "Penny, would you mind getting me a little something?"

"Not now, Kamal."

"Please?"

"I'm going to help Karina clear this stuff away first." Penny gestured at the candle and the herbs spread out over the dining room table.

"Fine." Kamal turned to Salina. He gave her a sly smile."

"Not a chance," Salina said. "You need to get back on your feet eventually."

"I think I'll go check on Amalia," Darshana said. "Make sure she's comfortable."

"I'll go with you." Mr. Kitaro smiled as he joined her.

"What's up with those two?" Kamal asked once they were out of earshot.

Penny shook her head. "I'm sure it's none of your business."

Karina placed the candle and herbs in a small box and stood. "I'll go put these away. I'm glad the spell worked."

"It was perfect, Karina." Penny gave her a nod. "Thanks for your help."

"I'm almost done with the translation of the scroll, too." Karina sighed. "It's just taking a little longer than I thought. But if my grandmother is feeling better tomorrow, maybe she can help too."

"That would be great." Penny nodded.

Karina left the room, and Penny raked her hands through her hair.

Kamal smiled and nodded. "We've got all the daggers."

"Yeah. Hard to believe." Penny said.

"I don't think I'll believe it until I see it with my own eyes," Salina added.

"Now we just need to—" The sound of glass breaking stopped him. He grabbed his crutches and stood from the dining room table. "What was that?"

A vision hit Penny. She let out a curse. It had somehow been blocked from her mind until now.

"The other four dark mages," she said. "They're here."

Kamal shifted, his grip tightening on his crutches. Salina jumped to her feet.

"And the Lotus," Penny whispered, her chest tightening with fear. "Naree is here."

She signaled for Kamal to keep quiet and then ran to the hall. Salina raced beside her. Throwing open Amalia's door, Penny stared wide-eyed at Darshana, Mr. Kitaro, Karina, and a sleeping Amalia.

"Don't make a noise," Penny said. "And don't open the door, whatever happens."

"Penny, what is it?" Darshana asked.

"I'll explain later."

"I'll stay with them," Salina said, closing the door.

Penny heard it lock. She raised her palms, aiming them at the door. A purple glow surrounded the door, and in the next second, it disappeared from sight. Invisible to whomever might come along.

As she ran back to the dining room, a thump and a scream stopped her in her tracks.

Again, she called upon her magic. This time she cloaked herself. She couldn't hold this magic very long, but she just needed to get to Kamal so she could hide him. And then she'd have to fight off the four dark mages—and, if it came to it, the Lotus—on her own.

When she reached the dining room, Kamal's crutches were sprawled out on the floor, and beside him—

"Kamal!" She let go of her magic.

There was a lot of blood. Kamal wasn't moving. Blood gushed from his chest. He'd been stabbed.

"No, no, no. Kamal."

He wasn't breathing. Penny began to hyperventilate.

Something clicked behind her, like shoes on the marble floor.

Before she could turn around to face the intruders, a cloth sack was shoved over her head. She screamed, but in the next second, something strong and hard struck her above her ear and the world faded to black.

The story continues in

SAPPHIRE MAGE

TURN THE PAGE
FOR A
PREVIEW OF
SAPPHIRE MAGE,
BOOK FIVE
IN THE
EMPIRE OF THE LOTUS
SERIES

One

Jae let out a sigh of relief when the cars finally reached the temple. He'd spent the entire drive checking the side mirror while Mayhara drove. He couldn't believe their luck; they hadn't been followed. Both cars had safely raced away from the celebrations at the governor's mansion before anyone could discover that the Pishacha and dark mages had been trapped in one of the rooms. Of course, the spell that had trapped them there had to have been broken by now. It had only lasted as long as Karina's enchanted candle burned. Which was why Jae's eyes had been trained on the road behind both getaway cars.

Mayhara shut off the engine once they were parked and glanced at Jae. Things were still tense between them, and Jae felt a vise tightening around his heart. She had been hurt because he hadn't disclosed the truth about his past relationship with Loni. She'd basically ended whatever had been growing between then before it could really even begin. He desperately wanted to find a time to sit down with her and explain himself. To tell her how he truly felt about her. But she continually brushed him off, stating that she needed to concentrate on their mission. Their relationship was purely professional now. Just two of the band of mages who vowed to protect the legacy of the Empire of the Lotus and prevent the dark god Kashmeru from destroying the world.

Shiro, who had been driving the other car, nodded to Jae once. The expression on his face was one of concern. Jae figured Shiro must have felt the same as he did about their escape from the party: uncertain and skeptical about their victory. They'd been successful acquiring the daggers, but that didn't mean the they'd won the battle. They still had to find and rescue Naree—Jae's sister, who was the reincarnation of the Lotus empress—and break the spell she was under. Kashmeru was controlling her every move, using the lure of their centuries-long, complicated, love-hate relationship to manipulate her to do his bidding. He needed her to break the spell that kept him locked in a cursed tomb. But he couldn't be released without the arcane daggers.

And the mages now had all seven.

Mayhara averted her gaze when Jae caught her looking at him. She turned and headed for the temple entrance without a word. Jae, Shiro, Yuki, and Loni followed. The skirts of the ball gowns Yuki and Loni wore swished as they walked.

But then, Yuki suddenly stopped.

Jae and Shiro turned to her when they noticed her standing frozen, her face pale against her auburn hair. The other mages stopped to study her as well. She wrapped her arms around her middle and shivered.

"What is it?" Jae asked. "What's wrong?"

"Fear." Yuki bit her lip. "I feel fear, coming from inside the temple. And… something else. I think it's…

death."

Jae and the others widened their eyes, their bodies tensing.

"Amalia," Mayhara said with panic in her voice. She turned on her heel and bolted into the temple.

Jae was close behind, the others in tow. He silently prayed to the gods that Amalia—the swamp witch who'd saved Shiro's life—was all right. Her blood had been poisoned by a dark mage, and despite Shiro's attempts at using his powers to syphon out the poison, Amalia was getting worse.

If she was dead…

The mages burst into the temple and began to search for the others who had stayed behind. But their search stopped short when Loni screamed in the living room. The rest of the mages hurried to find her.

Loni stood, trembling, with her hands covering her mouth and tears flowing down her cheeks.

Jae gasped at what was on the floor in front of her.

"Kamal!" Mayhara rushed to the body sprawled out on the cold marble floor surrounded by a pool of blood.

Jae bent down beside Kamal and immediately used his sapphire powers to listen for breathing or a heartbeat.

Neither one could be found.

"He's dead," Yuki whispered. "His spirit has left him."

As the diamond mage, Yuki would have been able to sense his spirit. If Jae had doubted himself about not hearing a pulse, he would have to believe Yuki's words.

"What… what happened here?" Shiro looked around.

The place was a shambles, furniture knocked over, drawers ripped from cabinets, and the sofa torn to shreds.

"They were here," Jae said. "They found the temple, and they were looking for the daggers."

"And killed Kamal in the process." Loni's voice broke on their fellow mage's name.

"Where are the others?" Mayhara stood and ran to the hall.

They all followed her to Amalia's room, but when they arrived at where her door should have been, they discovered it gone.

"What happened to her door?" Loni asked. "This doesn't make sense."

"Sight," Mayhara said, feeling the wall where the door used to be. "Penny must have cloaked the door with her amethyst powers."

Jae watched as Mayhara's hand clamped around a space of air.

"I found the knob." Mayhara jostled at it and then shook her head. "It's locked."

Yuki placed her hands on the invisible door, her palms glowing white. "They are in there. They're afraid. That's the fear I felt."

Jae lifted his palms, the blue glow reflecting off the wall where the door was hidden. He didn't know if Penny's cloaking spell had blocked the sound out, but he had to let the others inside Amalia's room know they were there.

"Hello, can you hear me? It's Jae." He pushed his sound powers through the wall. "Darshana? Penny? Salina? Are you in there?"

Still using his powers, he heard Karina—Amalia's granddaughter—swallow hard. The sound of a chair screeching against the floor followed.

"Jae! Yes!" Karina answered. "We're here."

"Can you unlock the door?" Jae asked. "Or is it spelled shut?"

In a few seconds, the lock clicked, and a wide-eyed

Karina opened the door, which magically materialized before their eyes.

The mages rushed inside. Mayhara first embraced a trembling Darshana and then Salina, Shiro crouched down next to the bed to feel the sleeping Amalia's forehead, and Loni asked Mr. Kitaro—the Sacred Key, keeper of one of the magic daggers—what had happened.

"We're not sure what happened," Mr. Kitaro said. "Penny told us to keep quiet and lock the door. We heard a lot of ruckus, but we followed her instructions."

Jae, Shiro, and Mayhara exchanged glances.

"They found the temple," Loni explained. "The Pishacha. Or the dark mages. Or both. And they… they killed Kamal."

Karina slapped a hand over her mouth and backed up against the wall. Darshana closed her eyes and bowed her head, her mouth drawn into a frown. Mr. Kitaro ran a hand down his face. Salina's jaw hung open in shock.

"They must have been searching for the daggers," Jae added.

"Wait." Mayhara's head whipped around. "Where's Penny?"

READ MORE OF SAPPHIRE MAGE

AVAILABLE November 10, 2020

From Snowy Wings Publishing

In case you missed them…

Be sure to check out first three books in the

Empire of the Lotus series:

Available from all online retailers

CRIMSON MAGE

http://books2read.com/crimsonmage

COPPER MAGE

http://books2read.com/coppermage

GOLDEN MAGE

http://books2read.com/goldenmage

Acknowledgements

I have wonderful groups of people who support me and cheer me on, and I don't think I could continue to write all my crazy story ideas without them. So a big thank you goes out to everyone who enjoys my twisted tales of magic and good vs. evil.

Thanks to my agent, Italia Gandolfo, and my editor, Amy McNulty, for always being there for me. And a grateful shout-out to my Snowy Wings gang and ARC team.

My home-base team—Bonnie, Sasha, Carol, and Rose—are the absolute best friends a weird girl like me could ask for. To my super-duper colleagues, Caroline, Sina, Viola, Winta, and Vango, I really appreciate your support. And to my family—Stephan, Kirsten, and Zachary—thanks for putting up with my days of not pitching in to clean up the house because I had to finish yet another chapter.

About the Author

 Dorothy Dreyer is a Philippine-born American living in Germany with her husband, her two college kids, and two Siberian Huskies. She is an award-winning, *USA Today* Bestselling Author of young adult and new adult books that usually have some element of magic or the supernatural in them. Aside from reading, she enjoys movies, binge-watching series, chocolate, take-out, traveling, and having fun with friends and family.

You can find out more about Dorothy on her website: http://dorothydreyer.com

Also from
Snowy Wings Publishing

WHEN DARKNESS WHISPERS

by Heather L. Reid

KILL ME ONCE, KILL ME TWICE

by Clara Kensie

ALL THE TALES WE TELL

by Annie Cosby

Find them and more at

https://www.snowywingspublishing.com/books